FAMILY OBLIGATIONS

END OF EARTH, BOOK 2

MATT SIMONS

Development Editing by Leon Unruh
Editing by The Pro Book Editor
Interior and Cover Design by IAPS.rocks

Wikimedia Foundation. (2023, March 29). 75th ranger regiment. Wikipedia. Retrieved April 3, 2023, from https://en.wikipedia.org/wiki/75th_Ranger_Regiment

eBook ISBN: 978-1-7378665-2-7
paperback ISBN: 978-1-7378665-3-4

1. Main category—Science Fiction/Time Travel
2. Other category—War & Military
3. Other category—Thrillers

First Edition

PROLOGUE

RULER

F INALLY, AFTER YEARS OF HARD work and the long hours in law school and then endless campaigning throughout this nation, I did it.

No, I must remain humble. *We* did it. There were so many who helped me get here.

Change is upon us in November of 2008. Next January 20, I will become the leader of the free world. I'll wave to the reporters and photographers on this historic moment and won't have to fake my smile.

I find the current president, George W. Bush, at the threshold of the White House front door. We engage in a firm handshake, and he says, "Congratulations, Mr. President-Elect."

I love the sound of that. "Thank you, George."

A Marine guard opens the door as George says, "Let me show you around. It'll be your home in nine weeks."

We walk down a hallway toward the West Wing.

"You're about to learn secrets that only the president is privileged to know. The Secret Service will show you the emergency protocols and hidden exits. Today, I'll be giving you information that only passes from president to president. Everything you will need to know before your inauguration. I know you want to end the war in Afghanistan, but things are not as simple as you think. Additional interests are invested in the war."

"I promised the people I would end the war," I say. "There are more important things than outside investments. It is time to end that quagmire and bring our troops home."

"It's not just about the money. This war justifies the current military budget, providing millions with work. The housing market is crashing, was never sustainable. The US economy will become completely dependent on military spending. Countless small companies build small parts that get shipped to big companies like Raytheon, who build the missiles we buy and use."

"I know how economics work, but there's a difference between profit and doing what is right."

George takes a deep breath and rubs his eyes. This job has aged him horribly. I remember when he was first elected eight years ago. His dark hair has turned completely white and all the color has drained from his skin, as if he has aged twenty years. He says, "Barrack, there is so much more at stake than just this nation. There are things in motion that cannot be stopped by us." He takes the tie off his suit and stuffs it into his pocket.

Aides move to the side of the hallway as we pass by, giving us privacy.

When we arrive at the Oval Office, George opens the door. "Welcome to your future office," he announces with a sweeping gesture.

As we step onto the deep carpet, I turn and admire the legendary room. "I have to say, I didn't picture you as a showman."

"It's all I've had to look forward to for a while now. Soon all my problems will be your problems and I can retire to my ranch back in Texas, never to worry about politics again. I think I'll try painting." He goes behind the desk, opens the top drawer on the left, and types numbers into a keypad. "You can change the code to whatever four digits you want. I use my wife's birthday, which also helps me remember to get her a gift."

George straightens as the wall opens to reveal a hidden stairwell where a bald man in a black suit and dark sunglasses stands. The man's presence feels off-putting even though he is a head shorter than me. The air grows unwelcoming as he approaches.

I ask, "Are you my future head of security?"

The man answers with a cold "No" as he shakes my hand with what feels like hard stone. "My name is Yabechun." He looks at George. "It's time. Did you tell him anything?"

Yabechun speaks with an unfamiliar accent, possibly European, but I can't narrow down the region.

George says, "It's best you explain everything instead of me."

Time for what? Why does George look so uncomfortable?

The stairwell leads to an underground conference room. A long table with eleven chairs, five on each side and a lone one at end. I assume the lone chair at the head of the table will be mine.

I don't like this feeling of unease. This guy is probably

going to brief me on something top secret regarding the military. I'll get to know who those additional interests are. I'm the leader of a country now. I must act like it, so I take the seat at the head of the table.

Sitting in the seat to my left, Yabechun places a black briefcase in front of me. Now with a closer view of this man's face, I can see the hard line that forms his jaw, as if his face had been chiseled from wood. He is completely hairless, no eyebrows or eyelashes. His skin is pail with no clear signs of age or scars, not even a mole or hint of acne. He removes his glasses, revealing blood red irises surrounded by white with oval pupils. Reminds me of goat eyes.

"You need to understand that you are a very small piece in a massive machine." He opens the case and takes out two folders, one thick with paperwork while the other is very thin. He hands me the thinner one first. "Let's get the simple stuff out of the way first."

Laying the file on the table, I open it and flip through its contents—eleven signed documents, each with a red fingerprint next to the signature. There is one blank document at the bottom of the pile. The documents are all the same, pledging undying loyalty to the ruler of the world. There are signatures dating back from President George W. Bush Jr. on January 9, 2001 to President Henry S. Truman on October 24, 1945.

Without looking up, I ask, "What is this?"

Yabechun says, "By signing and leaving your blood, you will here by swear your loyalty to me, same as your predecessors."

Jerking my head up, I stare him straight in the eyes. "Is this some kind of joke?"

Never breaking eye contact with me, Yabechun replies, "No. I wish it didn't have to be this way, but unfortunately, this is how it must be now. I'll put this into perspective. I am the man all world leaders bow down to. I decide what happens regarding foreign affairs as well as some domestic, but only if they have a major impact on the future. If I need your military, it will be provided. You do not have access to your nuclear launch codes because I do. I hold the launch codes to all nuclear-powered countries within the United Nations. I am the man who makes the decisions that impact the future because I will be the only one to live to see the results. Now if you will please sign so we can move on to what your role will be in making the future."

Looking over the document again, I say, "This can't be." I look to George. "Is this true?"

Bush shakes his head in confirmation.

"Then, why? Why are you in charge and not the leader of the free world? This nation is a symbol to the rest of the world, a beacon of hope and now change."

Maintaining a calm vainer, Yabechun answers, "Because humanity gave up its freedom to avoid total destruction. This is the only way we can move forward."

"And what if I don't sign?"

Yabechun snaps his fingers.

From the shadows, a Secret Service agent steps forward, cocks his pistol, and points it at the back of my head.

"Then I will have you killed and replaced within twenty-four hours with an actor who looks exactly like you. It truly is amazing how far plastic surgery has come. However, actors require so much more hand holding than politicians." He waves the agent away. "You see, the Secret Service doesn't work for you. They work for me. They will give their lives to protect you for their nation, but they will also take your life if it is for the good of humanity. So far, I've only had to replace one president." He turns to George. "Isn't that right, Philip?"

My body shakes with rage. "What?! That's not possible. I've known George since before he was president. I know his mannerisms. I've watched him age. Plastic surgery and acting can't change that. There would also have to be scars left over from the surgery."

The acting president turns his head to reveal a small scar behind his left ear.

All I can manage to say is, "When?"

God, I need to a smoke.

"Shortly after he was elected. I needed to have Saddam delt with publicly, with a full-scale war, and George didn't want his presidency to be defined by a war in the Middle East like his father's term had been. He was replaced, but a war still needs a reason. The country was too divided to willingly invade for a presidential assassination. Soldiers need to hate in order to kill. In the end, all it took was two buildings full of strangers in New York to send an entire nation willingly to war. I got what I needed as well as an extended war by an actor letting his vice profit from a broken operation."

He raises his arm up and points at me, his face and suit wrinkling from the movement. "As he wastes resources in burn pits only to request more!" He forces himself to stop, squeezing his hand shut. He then readjusts his suit before calmly continuing.

"But I digress. These actors are so well trained that no one can tell the difference, not even a spouse or a parent.

Now, swear loyalty to me and we can move humanity forward. I will introduce myself to the rest of your staff as the head of the United Nations and they will swear to secrecy about my existence, but it is important that you know what is to come. You are but a mortal man living on a tiny planet in a massive galaxy. There is so much more for you to understand."

After signing the paperwork, I prick my thumb with a needle and imprint it next to my name. "I need to know. Are you even human?"

As the man with red eyes places all the signed documents back into his briefcase, he says, "I was once, a long time ago, but there is more important work to do, so please don't disappoint me."

CHAPTER 1

ANGEL MOLINA

MY NAME IS ANGEL MOLINA, but in juvie, I'm just another a number. 11302007. It's the day I started my sentence. It hasn't been all bad. On Christmas, I got a frozen cookie, and I got a melted one for my thirteenth birthday. I don't get such luxuries at home. Now, after six months, my sentence is almost over.

It became miserably hot the second winter ended. Arizona only has two seasons, hot and kind of chilly. The concrete walls of this prison store the heat, turning this place into a massive oven. The air conditioning has never worked, and I bet it never will. The temperature is always miserable inside this place. A group of older teens use this time to exercise, or more accurately, prove how tough they are. All it does is add to the overall humidity of this ventless hall. Not that there's much to do to kill time otherwise. B-block is a long gray hallway with metal bunk beds lining the sides and fixed metal benches down the center. We live in a bland world.

I didn't get a job today on purpose, so I could engage in my favorite pastime, gambling with the addicts. They're always ready to bet in the vain hope of a buzz. We don't have much to bet with, just small amounts of money or personal items such as deodorant or cigarettes. I don't smoke, but cigarettes hold a lot of value. I can pay someone to clean the bathroom in my name for one cigarette, providing me with credit for none of the work.

The typical strategy everyone tries to use is to read your opponent for any indication of whether they have a good hand or not. Some people have obvious tells when they have a good hand. Freakin' Jacob smiles every time he has a face card. I think he has a crush on the queen. However, the majority in Juvie have walls up around their personality, making it hard to figure them out. It's much easier to just count how many cards are in play. Five players, including myself at the table in the center of the block. I like being close to my bunk. I can keep an eye on my stuff.

There's fifty-two in total, four different suits, each suit has three face cards, one ace and nine numbered cards. Shuffling eight times returns the deck. Everyone thinks more shuffles keeps the deck random, but it actually just returns it all back to where it was pre-shuffle. After two rounds of poker, I can accurately guess where each card is. It's all just a matter of math. I have a nine of hearts and the ace of spades. With the two cards in the center being a ten of spades and a king of diamonds, I know that the next card will be a nine of spades.

"Focus up, Angel!" someone yells suddenly as a thick textbook slams down in front of me, causing me to drop my hand of aces.

My bunkmate stands before me, sweating from another workout. He's been exercising multiple times every day for the past year. His muscles aren't exactly big, there are no weights to build bulk with. He uses his body as his weight, making his muscles dense and wiry. He's the same age as me, but his build makes him look older. He keeps his dark hair buzzed, and his eyes always look bloodshot from lack of sleep. I've seen him grab the tiny ledge of a door frame, then proceed to do twenty pullups with one arm before switching to the other arm to repeat the process. He makes me feel like a string bean by comparison. I'm no pushover when it comes to strength, I can hold my own in a fight, but I'm nothing compared to him. At least I have more facial hair than him. Even a peach fuzz mustache still counts.

"Really, Jason. More textbooks?"

Organizing the textbooks and writing utensils for a lesson, he makes sure I have a pencil with a good eraser before he plops down across from me and says, "We have work to do." He then pulls out a beat-up red notebook with a creased cover from him sleeping with it in his arms every night.

The others I was playing with drop their cards and take their winnings of bent cigarettes to continue the game at another table. Jacob takes a bit too long to gather his stuff as he trembles around Jason. He freezes when he sees Jason glaring at him, then in a panic, scurries away.

I say, "You don't have to scare them every time."

Opening his notebook Jason says, "There are more important things than others' feelings."

It's all about his formula for time travel, which I was hoping we could skip today. Reading about math and what it could build is a lot less fun than using it to win stuff, and I was about to win it all with my last hand.

I look over at him and say, "Jason, when I said I wanted to learn, I didn't mean I wanted to study it every day. I was in the middle of something, and I can't make any real progress if you keep interrupting."

He glares at one of the players coming back for his cards before rushing away again. Then he replies, "That's not important. You have what? A couple weeks left. I'm stuck here for the next five years. No one is going to target you with me around. This is something I can only show you for a limited time. Come on, let's get started."

I pocket my winnings, a handful of bent cigarettes. "Alright, Fine." He's lucky I find this stuff kind of interesting. But even so, I must ask, "Why are you so adamant about me learning this stuff? It's not like I can really do anything with just some formulas."

Jason opens his notebook to a page of mathematical equations. "Because it will save the world. You want to know how I know so much about time travel?"

I shouldn't have asked that. "Because you're from the future."

"Exactly! I have lived dozens of lives that have accumulated into this body." He takes a deep breath to compose himself. "I need your help to stop a war that will kill millions. Everyone here in B-block will have to fight in this war, and every single one of them will die. Angel, if you don't use this knowledge to make a difference, you will die in this war. I won't get out of here in time to stop it, but you can. Please…it's up to you."

"You've said that many times, but how am I, a thirteen-year-old Hispanic delinquent with only a month of lessons, supposed to stop *anything*?"

Jason smiles. "It's simpler than you think. Take the knowledge you learn from me to a college professor of physics, and they can guide you the rest of the way."

I try to protest, but he keeps talking, "You can't just hand him a notebook and walk away. You will need to prove this as your own work. They will have questions you must be able to answer. Plus, if you are the one in control of this knowledge, you will have a guaranteed life of luxury as the creator of a new technology. This technology will change everything, and I know it will stop the war. I have seen it."

A life of luxury does sound cool, and I just have to memorize some math. The dude who invented the car was one of the richest men to ever live. I will have a golden mansion full of servants to cater to me like a king. I give him a nod, and we get to work.

Going over the formulas again, I copy down the basics and then use them for problem solving to commit them to memory. One question burns in my head that I've wanted to ask since he first told me he was from the future. I've just been afraid of the answer. I figure it's now or never, so I ask, "Jason, you act like you knew me in the future. From the first time we met, you acted like we were close friends. I didn't know if that was your mind playing tricks on you after being in solitary for so long. And I wasn't going to turn down friendship from someone the big dogs feared. If you did actually know me in the future…what happens to me?"

He tenses as he grips the table. His veins bulge, and he grabs his head, holding it as if he's in a lot of pain. His headaches aren't getting any better. If I ask, he'll just brush it off like last time.

Then he unclenches and opens his eyes, wipes a small

amount of blood from his nose, and looks past me, his cold eyes seeming to see for miles. "You became a brave leader, willing to fight while others ran. You were stabbed to death in Baghdad. We couldn't stop the bleeding…" He pauses as if sorting out the memory. "We lost a lot of good people in that fight. That's why you have to make a change. You have the power to save us all."

"My God…" The words just fall from my mouth. Am I really that important? It all feels like too much for one person.

It takes us about thirty minutes to finish our review of the basics, then we go over the more complex applications of the equations.

I ask, "Yesterday you were talking about parallel universes. If you're from a parallel, then what's happening back there?"

Jason shrugs. "I have no idea. The last thing I saw was the light of a nuclear explosion. For all I know, the world descended into a nuclear holocaust. There are an infinite number of parallel universes existing at every moment in time. It is best to only worry about the one you're currently in. Otherwise, that can lead to some dark places. My travels through the timelines did damage to my brain that I know will lead to my death, but I wouldn't have been able to learn the exact calculation if I hadn't made the jump as many times as I did."

He draws a line on the paper with a circle on one end and a square on the other end. "The timeline is linear, or at least it appears to be. With a beginning and an eventual end. In the event of an extreme amount of energy is released. I call that the split."

He draws a perpendicular line in the middle of the original line, connecting to a new line parallel to the original with a square at the beginning. "This allows for a connection to a parallel universe. I've only experienced the connection to a parallel existing a few years before the split occurs again."

He draws another perpendicular line connecting to another parallel line. "This can go on forever unless a paradigm shift happens. This would need to be a large enough change earlier in the timeline to prevent the split from ever happening. This change will be your use of this technology."

I keep thinking of myself as the chosen one. It's like I've been chosen by destiny.

An hour or so later, the lesson ends when our head corrections officer, Mr. Brook approaches. A massive man with a thick mustache to make up for his comb over, he towers over us as he says, "Jason Baker and Angel Molina. What are you boy's working on?"

His large size intimidates everyone. I once saw him stop a fight by throwing both fighter's to opposite ends of the hall at the same time. Just picked them both up by the chest of their shirts and flung them like dolls.

Without hesitation Jason says, "Math."

"That's good, build a strong mind. Well, sorry to interrupt your math, but, Angel Molina, it's time for your hearing. One last interview before your release."

Jason tells me, "Give 'em hell, but don't be a dick."

Mr. Brook escorts me to the office building at the front of the Juvenile Detention Complex. I am offered a lone seat in front of Warden Fox and four other adults I kind of recognize. This is probably the second time I've seen the warden. He hides in his office all day unless there's an emergency. Having trimmed his mustache and goatee since I saw him last, he looks like Colonel Sanders, and I try not to smile. The two adults on his right are the resident psychologist, Ms. Gee, and Mr. Brook takes his seat next to her. But I don't know the two on Fox's left. Each one has a stack of papers they are writing on. My best guess is that they're from the district attorney's office, there to hear if I deserve to go home.

Warden Fox speaks first. "How are you today, delinquent 11302007?"

"I'm fine."

The district attorney's representative says, "You received a rather light sentence for your offenses. We wanted to see if you remembered where the drugs in your bag came from."

I ain't no snitch. "Like I told the cop and his crazy dog, I don't know. I probably switched bags with someone on the bus without realizing it."

All five of them write that down.

Mr. Brook says, "Angel, you seem to be a smart kid. You've already felt the consequences of your actions. If you *mix up* bags again, you'll be put away for the next five to ten years. You don't want to end up like your friend Jason Baker or your cousin David Luna. Jason is too violent to ever live a normal life, while your cousin keeps taking what doesn't belong to him. Think about what you want for your life. Understand?"

Really? Ten goddamn years! Just for some fucking weed. Better say only what they want to hear. "I understand."

That night I lie awake in my bed. I can't sleep but not because of the heat this time. There's just so much. I'm almost out. I know Dad will have me go back to work for him, moving product. I don't want that life anymore, but can I really cause a difference large enough to change the future? No, that's how Jason looks at it. I need to look at it my way. What could this do for me? What do I want? I'm always doing errands for Dad. Taking his packages to his friends. There's been so many since Mom and Dad split up. I hardly even attended school last year. I do want to learn more. I want to build things, even if I don't know what to build. Maybe I should try to live with Mom.

I hear a yell from the bottom bunk and lean over to see what it was just as Jason rolls onto the floor and begins doing push-ups. Of course, his crazy exercise routine. That dude has never slept through an entire night. There has to be something wrong with his brain, or maybe it really is a side effect of time travel.

Mom does live in Phoenix. I could take the notebook to a college professor there. Sell the equations for a good chunk of cash. Set myself up for a life of luxury. Then again, it would piss off Dad if I stopped doing his errands. But maybe once he sees my new wealth, then he would finally show me some appreciation.

For the final week before my sentence ends, I am taken to a different portion of the facility to avoid possible attacks by spiteful delinquents. On the way, Mr. Brook lets me say goodbye to my cousin in the infirmary who was stabbed a little over a month ago. Jason saved his life and beat the shit out of his attacker. Jason really has done a lot for me. Maybe we were good friends in that parallel life he keeps talking about.

I enter the infirmary with a guard close by and walk over to David's hospital bed. He's watching a small TV in a cage with a distorted broadcast. He should have recovered by now, but the wound got infected from the dirty shiv. I say, "Que pasa?"

David's voice is weak, but he fights through it. "Hurting, everywhere. So, they're finally letting you out?"

I nod. "I'm a free man."

He says, "Listen, I'm going to make a full recovery. Don't worry about me. I ain't going to let this stop me. When I get out, we're going to celebrate!" He winces as he talks. I think the blade pierced his lung.

I imagine us partying in my golden mansion. "I can't wait."

We almost high five but then switch to bumping knuckles after he misses my hand. He moves slow, and I hit his hand a bit too hard. David plays it off like it didn't hurt. I don't like seeing him like this, but I know he will be fine.

The time finally comes for me to leave. I walk through the last locked door. The first building of Juvie is a clean, office-style room with new carpet and padded chairs of bright colors. It is a stark contrast to the bland world I've been living in. Jason stands in handcuffs with several guards next to Warden Fox. Jason is allowed to say goodbye to me, but they still don't trust him. He gives me my notebook with all my attempts to copy his work, which I can't believe I almost forgot. He also gives me his original red notebook and says, "Make it your own. You have till December of 2012 to make a difference. I believe in you."

Five years. I take the books. "I'll do what I can." I want the easy life.

Warden Fox opens the door and two guards help me leave the juvenile detention facility. I collect my civilian clothes along with everything I had when I was arrested, minus the bag of drugs. It feels good to change out of the orange jump suit. Then the gates open to a vast desert by a quiet freeway.

Mr. Brook puts out his hand, saying, "Best of luck to you. Stay clean, and you won't have to come back."

My grip is overpowered by his far larger hand. "I don't plan on it." I guess Warden Fox couldn't be bothered to say goodbye.

Then I get on a bus that takes me back home to Yuma. The bus driver is plugged into headphones like there is no point in worrying about security around one former delinquent on his way home.

I zone out, just watching the empty desert pass by the window. Miles of endless cactus, dead bushes, and sand. I'm not tired enough to sleep, so I just stare. Two hours later, the bus pulls into the Juvenile Court and Detainment Center of Yuma where I am brought to a large waiting room. It is a different feeling to be here after spending time in Juvie. This place feels more open and shinier. Only one person guards the front door. The air conditioning actually works. I start to shiver in my shorts and sleeveless shirt. I move to sit near the door where I get a breeze of hot air every time the door opens. I'm sure Dad will be here soon.

An hour passes. Then two hours. On the third hour, I figure I can take a bus home.

I go for the exit, but the guard stops me. "You can't leave without a parent or guardian present to sign you out."

"My padre probably got stuck at work. I can just take a bus."

The guard replies, "I can't let you leave without a parent or guardian present to sign you out."

"Don't make me sit here all day."

"I can't let you—"

I cut him off by mimicking his voice to sound as stupid as possible. "Without a parent or guardian present. I heard you the first time. Is there at least anything decent here to read, other than old magazines that should've been thrown away years ago?"

The guard says, "I'm not paid to know that."

With all the sarcasm I have, I thank him for the help. There's nothing left to read but Jason's notebook.

As I dive in, I realize it's a lot easier to read about the impending doom of the third world war without Jason talking over my shoulder. The most impressive part is how simple he wrote out the concepts. He broke everything down to its simplest root and slowly expanded on each aspect of time travel and the impacts of parallel realities. The equations prove exactly how everything is connected through energy and breaks the energy down to a vibrational frequency. He even figured out the exact level of power the frequency needs to be at.

Could this be achieved with just a couple of speakers? No, or someone would have built it years ago. What if I blended frequency with pure electricity? Jason did say it would take a nuke to send him back to our time. I will need a lot of power to achieve what is necessary to open a parallel universe.

More time passes as my stomach growls at me. Is there any food around here? Looking around, I see the two vending machines, one full of snacks and one for drinks. The snacks have already been picked clean, leaving few options. I have enough money for food or enough for the bus home. Then again, there is the possibility that there's no food at home. Wouldn't be the first time the cupboards were empty.

I could pull a fire alarm and sneak out. Unfortunately, there aren't any fire alarms within reach. I could blend into a large family and sneak out with them, if there were any large groups left. I missed that opportunity hours ago. Only I and the people who work here remain. My best bet is to wait for Dad to come pick me up. So I decide I might as well buy some old junk food to fight this hunger.

Eventually, closing time comes along and there's still no sign of Dad. I try to leave again, but the guard stops me. "I'm sorry, but I can't let you leave without a parent—"

"Or guardian. I know, but this place is closing. What else can I do? My padre never came."

The guard talks into his radio. "Jean, there is a delinquent here no one picked up. What should I do?"

I can't hear the reply through the radio static, but I know what's coming. "Come on, man, I already served my time. Don't make me stay here."

The guard places his hand on my shoulder and escorts me into the facility. "Just come with me."

"Son of a bitch."

I am checked into a cell block with all the other runaway kids. The block has ten cells down a hallway with a long table and benches in the middle. To the right is a small half-basketball court surrounded by high concrete walls and a chain link roof. There's a supervisor's desk next to the only door in or out. Five of the cells have lights on in them. Looks exactly like the unit I was in when I was first met Jason. He almost strangled a kid that day for pushing me.

The supervisor signs some paperwork, her dark hair in a tight bun that's starting to fall apart. Must have been a hectic day.

I ask, "Hey, is there any food left over? I haven't really eaten all day."

She shows no concern. "There won't be any more chow until morning. You should have said something thirty-five minutes sooner."

I try to catch a glance into the passing cells. I see nothing in the first cell, but in the second is a kid sitting on the edge of the bed, folding a piece of paper into a plane.

The supervisor of the cell block says, "Keep your eyes forward. You will meet everyone tomorrow."

My cell's bed is a lumpy mattress on a concrete slab built out.

The supervisor says, "The door stays locked. At 7 a.m., I expect you up with everyone else and the bed to be made. Understood?"

"This ain't my first time."

After the door closes with a clang, I curl up on the familiar feeling bed with the notebooks in my arms. My stomach growls at me all night long.

Finally, morning comes followed shortly by warm food. I devour everything, almost chocking on a slice of bread. The kid across from me looks horrified. He's the one who was making paper airplanes last night. This kid is covered in sunburns. Is this white boy judging me? If he makes any kind of move, I can't back down.

I tense up, remembering how viciously Jason would fight.

Then the kid offers me his pudding cup.

I snatch it out of his hand before he can change his mind.

He says, "I get it, man. I was almost starved when I got here, but that was my own fault. What are you in for?"

I force down a cup of water to clear my throat. "I already served my time. I'm just waiting for a ride out of here. The stupid rules require a parent or a guardian to sign you out."

"I ain't in trouble either. I got picked up out in the desert. They thought I was a runaway. It was just survival training."

This guy has to be least two years younger than me. "Training? There's nothing in this desert but rocks."

"That's how it appears to the untrained eye. But there's a lot of life out there to survive on. Plenty of snakes and lizards as long as you know how to properly eat them. Even tarantulas are edible. The difficult thing is water, but I had plenty of that. Enough for three days. Four, if I was smart about it."

I'm getting a creepy feeling from this kid. "You were surviving for three days out in the desert. Why?"

He smiles. "Because all my brothers had done it. It was my turn. My family has a motto. To be born a Kane is to be born a killer." He sits up straight at that. "And I plan on taking that skill into the military like my father before me and his father before him."

This guy is nuts, but it's better to have the nutcase on your side. I learned that with Jason. "Kane…that is a hell of a motto to live up to. You got a first name?"

He puts out his hand, dry with small cuts all over it. "Austin."

We shake. "Angel." I bet this kid is going to be a serial killer someday. "How long you been here?"

Austin says, "I got picked up yesterday. My family are up in Perryville for my aunt's execution. They'll get me on their way back."

What the fuck did he just say? "Your aunt's execution? What did she do?"

Austin continues like this is a normal conversation. "She murdered like ten people to steal their homes and sell them. My dad thought this was a perfect time to start my survival training."

What the hell is wrong with this kid's family? I thought my family was fucked up with my father selling drugs and my mother abandoning me.

A day passes as I wait at the Juvenile court. Austin is the closest to my age, and there is one kid younger than us who doesn't talk or look at anyone. I think I was like that the first time I ended up here. The two others are teenagers who are glued to each other at the hip. My guess is they're partners in crime and they probably got busted together. I think, *You two better pray you end up in the same joint, or you're screwed.*

Come on, Dad, where are you? He has to know my sentence ended. The people in charge said they tried to contact him, but he had yet to answer any phone calls. Does he not care? How could he just forget about me? If he doesn't come and get me, they could put me into foster care. Do they have Mom's number?

Then a guard comes into the cell block and calls out, "Austin Kane. Your parents are here to take you home."

Austin marches out with robotic movement, showing no sign of emotion as he leaves.

You know what, I'm kind of glad he's gone. I mean he was nice and all, but that kid is a ticking time bomb. At least his parents care enough to come get him. Is he afraid of getting punished for getting caught? That's probably why my dad hasn't gotten me. This is my punishment for getting caught, but surely I've paid the price already. I spent six months in Juvie surrounded by violent offenders. If it wasn't for David and Jason's protection, I would've become a victim. As it was, David almost died.

CHAPTER 2

HOME

AFTER ANOTHER NIGHT OF SLEEPING on a sour mattress, locked in a small room with a solid steel door, and watching other kids come and go, I continue to wait. Where are you, Dad? I shoot some hoops on the half court outside with three other kids as we see who can make the longest shot.

Midmorning, a guard enters the cell block with official looking paperwork. "Angel Molina. Your father is here to take you home."

I knew he wouldn't forget. I sprint to the guard so quickly I almost run into him. They escort me back to the lobby where sits a man resting his arms on his gut as he franticly texts on a flip phone. His thick glasses and greasy mustache reflect the phone's light. His mustache makes him look like he is always frowning.

The guard says, "Renato Molina, here is your son."

My dad says, "About time! I've fallen way behind thanks to you."

He towers over me at six feet, weighing over three hundred pounds. He used to be a Marine but hasn't worked out a day since his discharge. He grabs my hand and pulls me out of the building. There are no words between us as we drive away in his dented old Volvo. Renato just grumbles to himself. I turn on the radio to combat the silence, but every station is playing a commercial at the same time. I stop on the least obnoxious sounding one about pizza. Having left before lunch, my stomach growls.

"Renato, where are we going?" If we were going home, we would have made a right two lights ago. Maybe we're going somewhere to celebrate my release.

"I have to make a few stops. Picking you up threw me off schedule."

"Do any of these stops involve pizza?"

Renato's phone buzzes. "Shit! I am way behind." He quickly texts back with one hand on the wheel.

Eventually we arrive at a red brick house surrounded by chain link fencing, with black metal bars covering all the windows and doors.

Renato hands me a bag from the back seat. "I have to make another delivery. You take care of this one."

"I don't really want to do that anymore. Last time I sold your stuff, I got attacked by a police dog. I just got released. This feels too much like tempting fate."

He shoves the bag into my stomach and pushes me against the door. "If you don't do this, you're not going to eat today. This is how I support us, and if it needs to get done, you need to get it done!" He reaches to open the door, dumping me onto the street with the bag in my lap. "I'll be back in ten. Don't let them shortchange you."

I slam the door closed, and he drives off.

"Asshole." I brush myself off as I walk up to the fence.

The doorbell is next to the front door, which is past an iron security door locking in the porch. I think they over did it. The gate screeches, and I open it only enough to squeeze through, then close it behind me. I'm almost to the security door when I hear a loud bark and the sound of four feet speeding toward me. I jolt forward, almost slipping as a large pit bull rounds the corner of the house. Its eyes glow with hatred at the intruder.

No time to pray, I jump the last few steps and grab the handle, praying aloud, "This door better be unlocked." I rip the iron security door open and then slam it behind me just as the beast lunges.

Barking and jumping against the door, it tries to push its large head through the small cracks.

My heart is beating in my ears. "Not this time, bitch."

A woman shouts, "Who the hell are you?"

I spin around to face a large middle-age woman covered in tattoos, then fall back into my old routine. "I'm Renato's son. He couldn't make it, so I'm making the delivery."

The door shakes with the dog still barking and jumping into it.

The lady yells, "Shut up! Daisy!" but the beast keeps barking. The lady pushes me aside and kicks the metal door, knocking the animal off it. "Shut up!" As the dog stops barking and wonders off, she turns her attention back to me. "So you're the delivery boy today? Fucking typical of Renato to push responsibility onto someone else. Wait here." She leaves me alone in this small space.

There isn't much to look at, just a concrete path with colored pebbles on the sides. Then the realization hits me that Renato never told me what I was supposed to give her or how much she had to pay.

I open the bag. There has to be some kind of label on this stuff. Renato is meticulous about what he grows. Ten ziplock bags with Purple Punch written on them in black Sharpie. Now I have a point of reference. Last time I sold Purple Punch, it was a hundred bucks an ounce. Knowing Renato, each bag holds exactly an ounce.

The lady returns with a shoe box wrapped in duct tape. "You got two ounces of Purple Punch?"

"Only if you've got two hundred bucks."

Stone-faced, she opens the box while keeping me from seeing inside it.

Why doesn't she want me to see into the box? Fear creeps up the back of my neck. She could be reaching for a gun. Is that why Renato didn't want to make this delivery? Everything slows down. If she pulls out a gun, I'll have a second to smack it away with the bag. I can use that time to get out the door and over the fence. Hopefully she won't risk gunning me down in the middle of the street.

I shift my stance for a quick escape. Then I hear a happy sound of nonsense from inside the house. I see a toddler beyond the open door, can't be older than two.

The lady says, "Raising kids is stressful." She pulls out a stack of twenties and counts them out.

Without relaxing, I give her two bags.

She accepts them and turns back to her house.

"Wait, what about Daisy?" I look over my shoulder nervously.

"Don't worry about her. She's all bark no bite." She disappears inside, closing the door behind her.

I am not falling for that. Once the backpack is zipped up and secured, I sprint across the yard. Without bothering to open the gate, I swing myself over the fence just as the dog returns in a fury. Landing safely on the sidewalk, I stand waiting for my ride while the dog barks at me with all of its hate.

After forty minutes of waiting on the sidewalk, Renato finally comes back. He counts the money before I am allowed into the car. Not even a thank you.

"So, are we stopping for food?" I ask.

"Oh yeah, I got some McDonalds." He points to a white paper bag in the back.

I reach back and grab the bag. It contains a couple of scattered French fries and a cold burger with no condiments beneath two crumpled Big Mac wrappers.

Eventually we arrive at a small house with air conditioning units on every window and Renato parks in front of the garage. The front yard has patches of overgrown dead grass. He makes sure the garage door is secure before he unlocks the front door. Upon entering the house, I'm hit by a smell closely resembling a skunk. Home at last. The living room looks like a jungle with plants connected to a hydroponic watering system under lots of bright blue lights. I don't think I've been able to sit in the living room since Mom left. It doesn't matter now though. All I care about is sleeping in my own bed. But when I open the door to my room, I find all the furniture gone and nothing but marijuana plants growing in every corner.

"Where's my bed?"

Renato yells from the kitchen, "Out back."

This is what I come home to? I go back to the kitchen,

my anger boiling over. "You destroyed my fucking room for more plants?"

Renato's massive figure looms far above me as his voice deepens while delivering my only warning. "Don't you dare say *your room*, boy. This is *my* house! All these rooms are *my* rooms!" He moves closer to me. "There are plants in *my* room because they pay the bills. Because those plants bring in more money than you. You damn parasite."

I should back down and accept that I'll be sleeping outside. It wouldn't be the first time. But I am *not* a parasite, not after everything I have done for him. "Are you fucking kidding me! I just spent six months locked up in Juvie because I was moving *your* product! I bring in just as much as you. For fuck's sake, I take more of the risk than you! I almost got eaten by a fucking dog today!" With the rage built up from all those long nights in captivity, I push him with all my might.

He doesn't budge. I might as well have pushed a mountain.

Suddenly I'm knocked off balance, and my face burns. Did he just slap me? Then his hand swings back, and I can't block fast enough. My stomach erupts as his fist impacts my gut. I crumple to the floor, unable to breathe. I try to inhale but vomit spews out. I don't have time to recover before he drags me across the tile floor and throws me out the front door. While I try to gather myself, I feel a hard kick to my side that launches me into the front yard. Dead weeds crumble into sharp sticks as they catch me. Coughing hard, I try to hold back my tears, but it's no use. Everything hurts too much. I slowly roll out of the dead plants and begin to stand up just as my bag from Juvie flies at me, knocking me back down.

Renato yells, "You're nothing, and you will remain nothing! You can live outside until you are more valuable than my plants." Then he slams the door closed.

I've given up so much for him, but he doesn't care. I try to yell, "Fuck you, old man!" My words come out as a whimper. What's the point?

The tears break through. They sting as they cross my swollen cheek. How could Mom leave me with him. Do they both hate me that much? I hate feeling so weak, but where else can I go? Doing anything about this, trying to get help of any kind, would only land me in foster care, or worse, back in Juvie.

CHAPTER 3

BACK TO NORMAL

I WAKE UP IN THE BACKYARD to the sound of old brakes screeching. Glancing past the end of the house, I see a yellow school bus stopped to pick up a group of teenagers. I lay back down, resting my head on my duffle bag. Last night I found my mattress wrapped in plastic, leaning against the back wall next to my dresser. I didn't bother unwrapping it, not wanting to touch the mold growing on it. Unlike the front yard, there are no dead plants behind the house, only dirt protected by a tall brick wall. My neck feels stiff, so I try not to move it too much. I barely slept as it didn't cool off until around two in the morning. Feeling gross, I use the hose in the backyard to clean myself as well as quench my thirst. Why does hose water taste better than any water I had in Juvie? I shake the bugs out of some clothes from my dresser and change.

Then I just sit on the porch with nothing to do, so I take the notebook out of my bag. How the hell am I going to make any of this happen? It all feels too big for me.

Renato unlocks the back door to give me a backpack and

a burner phone. He says, "The addresses are in the phone. Trash it before you get back."

I guess I'm back to the old routine then. I have a dozen things I would like to say, as well as throw this backpack right at him, but that would only result in another beating. I ask, "Is there anything for breakfast?"

He says, "Sure, wherever you can find it," before closing the door.

Yeah, it's right back to normal. Thankfully, when Renato moved my dresser to the backyard, he didn't go through it. I find my secret stash of cash inside my sock drawer. About twenty bucks in small bills that I pocketed from various deliveries. Renato is stingy, making sure he's made the exact amount for each bag, but that doesn't stop me from up-charging a bit when I know I can get away with it. I have to survive somehow.

I make my way to the Quickie Mart at the end of the neighborhood on the main road. I'll be able to catch a bus into town. I buy some Pop-Tarts and a cold water. The clerk is a man in his early fifties named Frank.

"Angel? Where have you been?" His voice bursts with joy.

"Doing time."

He shakes his head with disappointment. "I thought you were smart."

"I am, just wasn't fast enough."

He laughs at that.

I leave as another customer comes in. I take the bus to a neighborhood in between the two parts of the local Marine base. It's cheap housing, so a lot of military members live there. I have the area completely mapped out in my head.

From what I have gathered from the pictures in the house and the few stories I have heard about Renato, he was dishonorably discharged from the Marine Corps for selling drugs. He met Mom sometime before he was discharged. Most of his customers are former associates or come recommended. It turns out that people in a highly stressful line of work like to self-medicate. Renato provides everything they want and can't legally get.

In the phone are instructions for each sale. Some I call or text before making the drop in person. Some leave money in spots hidden around the front yard. Money stowed under plants to be replaced with a bag of weed. The neighborhood is always quiet on a school day.

It is also miserably hot. I have to sit in the shade for a minute to cool off. Sweat burns my eyes, and my stomach throbs. One day I'm going to live somewhere where it is never hot. A place far in the mountains, surrounded by tall trees. I hate this empty desert. I hate this never-ending heat. I hate that I have to work all day out here while everyone else gets to live a normal life.

What can I do? This is all I know. I'll probably do this for the rest of my life until a delivery goes bad and I'm shot dead. As I take my warm water from my bag, I see Jason's red notebook. I must have packed it without thinking.

"I have no future," I say, shoving it back into the bag.

After a long day of walking and down to my last bag of weed, I count my cash to ensure it is what Renato will be expecting. Then I see a black and white car pass me by and quickly shove the money in my pocket. The police car makes a U-turn. I have to fight the impulse to run. They don't know shit. Running will only make it worse. I'm just a kid who got out of school an hour early. I walk casually as if nothing is wrong. I know of a gap between some houses not far away that leads to a wash where I can disappear into the desert.

The police car slows down next to me and the cop calls out, "Shouldn't you be in school?"

I turn my head to see a young cop with large biceps. Then I see K-9 Unit written on side of the vehicle as a dog starts to bark from the passenger's seat.

Stay calm. The dog may know, but the cop doesn't.

I say, "I got out early."

Then the dog jumps over the cop, out of the open window at me.

I immediately start running.

The cop yells, "Hey, stop!"

I don't know if it was directed at me or the dog. As the jingling of the dog's collar grows closer, gaining on me, I grab a wall to instantly turn down an alleyway. The dog thuds into the alley wall, stopping only for a second, and the cop is close behind.

My stomach burns so bad that I can't run at full speed. I knock down a full garbage can to slow them down. Hearing stumbling behind me, I am relieved that bought me some distance, but I need to lose them. The alley has been closed off with a chain link fence and razor wire, but there's a small space between the fence post and the wall that's just wide enough for me to slip through. I take off my backpack without slowing down, suck in my stomach, and slide through. But as I am about to pull the pack through, the police dog grabs it with sharp teeth and refuses to let go. The pack is probably covered with the stank of marijuana just from being in Renato's house. I try to pull it away, but the dog's jaw is locked. I pull with all of my might. "Let go, you stupid mutt!"

The cop comes up, breathing hard but still with some fight in him.

In an instant, I can see what will happen. The cop will catch me and I'll go right back to Juvie for the next six years. I'll never know what it's like to live a normal life. And if Jason's right, I'll die before I turn nineteen. I take my notebook out of the pack, then let go and run into the wash.

CHAPTER 4

PARADIGM SHIFT

B Y THE TIME THE BUS gets me back to my neighbor-hood, the sun has almost set. I can't keep living in fear. I have to face Renato, and more importantly, I have to win. I'm not strong enough to face him head on.

With the notebook in hand, I take a deep breath and then dial 911 on the burner phone.

A dispatcher says, "911. What's your emergency?"

I raise my voice to sound hysterical. "There's a domestic disturbance!" I give them Renato's street address. "The man sounds drunk, and he's got a gun!"

The dispatcher says, "Stay on the line. Police are on their way."

I shout, "Please hurry!" I take my head away from the phone and scream in as high a pitch as I can. "Oh god! He's going to kill them!"

"Stay where you are. Don't involve yourself. Police are on their way."

"I hope so."

I smash the phone on the ground and kick it into a

storm drain. No more evidence on me. I set the notebook down by the front gate. God, I don't want to do this, but I knock on the door anyway. "I'm back!"

Renato opens the door. "Where's the money?"

I hand him the cash.

He lets me in as he counts. "You're fifty bucks short."

It doesn't matter how honest of a mistake it was, the response would be the same.

"I lost it." I try to say more, but Renato smacks me across the face with an open palm.

He yells, "You are absolutely useless!"

I look him right in the eyes for the first time in years. "I am far more useful than you, you miserable old bastard!"

He punches me with all of his force.

I black out for a moment, then realize I'm on the ground. The world is blurry. Renato yells more degrading insults at me while I try to sit up, wiping the blood from my nose.

I say, my body trembling, "I have done everything you have ever asked! But nothing is ever enough. You hurt me because I can't fight back. You're pathetic!"

Renato picks me up by one arm, yanking my shoulder out of its socket. I feel more pain than I have ever felt before and scream uncontrollably. Then he throws me again. Each roll sends more pain through my body until I crash into the fence. He kicks me hard in the gut while I'm down, knocking all the air out of my lungs. Then he kicks me in the ribs, and I feel them break. I see bright red lights. Am I dying?

Someone yells, "Freeze, dirt bag!"

I start to giggle through my tears, then my giggle slowly turns into a laugh. I am in immense pain, but I know for once it's going to be alright. I look at Renato through my one unswollen eye.

He glares down at me and calls me a "fucking rat."

I force myself to stay awake, not wanting to miss what comes next. "You forgot to close the door, fucker." I smile with the taste of blood in my teeth.

Renato tries to run, but the cops hit him with a taser. While he's stunned, another cop equal to Renato's size tackles him with the force of a semitruck. Another cop kneels beside me to give first aid, trying to treat my injuries.

I feel around for the familiar paper pages of my notebook and pull it close as I watch Renato lose a fist fight to a team of cops with batons.

CHAPTER 5

THE KANE FAMILY

MY NAME IS BARRY KANE. I am the second son of Colonel William Kane. I am destined for greatness, as every Kane is born to be a killer, but instead, as the second son, I am tasked with the chore of cleaning the pool in this desert heat.

Thankfully it's a dry heat, unlike when we lived in Florida, where the weather was at least interesting when hurricane season came around. I remember when Dad said he was being transferred to the Marine Corps Air station in Yuma and promised the house would have pool. Sounded good to me. That meant we would finally live off post. I did not anticipate having to clean it every day though.

My brothers were excited about moving here until they saw the endless rocks and sand. I can go out whenever I want without having to get through a guarded gate. To be honest, I wish we had moved back to North Carolina. I want to have a snowball fight. Rock fights aren't the same.

My brother John yells from the porch, "Are you done yet?"

"I'm working on it! It would get done faster if you helped." This is not how I wanted to spend the last few days of spring break, rushing through chores before my aunt's execution. She put her family on the list, allowing us to witness it, and The Colonel has been adamant about us going. When I first heard, I pictured a firing squad, but only Utah does that. Arizona only executes people by lethal injection. The last woman executed in Arizona was publicly hanged and they miscalculated the rope length, making it too long and resulting in her being decapitated. That sounds more interesting than death by needle.

Just as I finish my last lap around the pool, taking out rafts of pollen from our neighbor's mesquite tree, I hear a small splash. Looks like a lizard fell in and is splashing all about in a panic. I scoop it out with my skimmer and gently place it on patch of grass, then lean down for a good look. It's a wide lizard covered in spikes. I've heard of these. I think they're called horny toads. Horny toad, kind of a dumb name. I wonder what the scientific name is. It bursts into a run and ends up right back in the pool.

I don't bother with the pool net this time. I scoop it out with one hand, then cover it with the other until I can place it on the brick wall surrounding our backyard. "This time it's up to you."

"You done yet!"

"Yeah!" I take one last look at the horny toad as it jumps off the wall, back into the yard.

I hear Mom say, "I told you to go get him, John. I could have just yelled for him."

John says, "Sorry, I thought that's what you meant."

Moms turns her attention to me. "Go put on some nice

clothes. Long pants without holes in them. No shirts with band logos on them either, and please comb your hair. We need to look presentable."

I got Mom's curly blonde hair that naturally parts around my face, and I keep it longish while my brothers keep their brown hair buzzed like The Colonel. I know I'll have to buzz it off after high school, so I'm going to enjoy it for now.

Mom is wearing the same black dress she wore to Grandpa's funeral. My big brother is wearing his new military uniform. Fresh back from his first deployment and he has to go to our aunt's execution. The Colonel insisted on it. What was it he said? "It's something we must do as a family."

Just before the staircase, I pass The Colonel's office, full of pictures spanning his military service and his favorite picture of my grandfather and great grandfather's reunion in Bastogne framed next to his office door. My grandfather looks miserable in his dirty airborne uniform with an unkept beard, but my great grandfather has a massive smile and a brand new army outfit with a Colt .45 Peacemaker on his hip and his unmistakable scar on his left cheek. One line stretches upward from his chin to his ear while another scar crosses it from his eye down his cheek and there's a small scar on his lower eye lid. It looks like an apostrophe X. Surprisingly, there are a lot of pictures of my great grandfather in the office. The earliest one is from 1916, of him in his French Foreign Legion uniform and he's about sixteen years old. He apparently lied about his age to join. He only has the apostrophe scar just under his left eye, but he'll receive the X before the end of the first world war. Next to that is a newspaper article about my great grandfather as he arrests a notorious crime boss, titled "Jack Kane Brings Justice Back to the Streets of Chicago" and dated 1930. He stood proud as he posed for the cameras, always with that Colt Peacemaker on his hip. The Colonel keeps that gun in his safe and claims it's still in working condition, but I've never seen it fired.

I hear The Colonel going over a checklist with my little brother. "Gallon of water."

Austin's voice cracks. "Check."

"Medical kit?"

"Check."

"Three days' worth of food?"

"Check."

"Excellent. Remember that food is a backup if you can't scavenge. Now Mom wants you to have her cell phone, but don't use it unless you get into real trouble."

He says, "Yes, sir!" with excitement.

The Colonel has gotten so much nicer. I had to survive in a Florida swamp with half that number of supplies and no phone. I had to eat grasshoppers for three days. They had a bitter crunch and the taste still haunts me, but I learned how to survive those swamps. Stay in the water, away from the thick mud, which can make you a target for the alligators. I had to sleep in a tree to stay safe.

According to Arizona State Laws, Austin is too young to witness an execution despite The Colonel's intense arguing. Instead, he gets to do his survival test. What a shame, because this is a once in a lifetime opportunity.

I put on the only collared shirt I own, a black button-up, and the only pair of blue jeans I have that doesn't have a hole in them. They're a half inch short, exposing my ankles. According to The Colonel, "This is not a day to look like a punk." Though shorts would be way more comfortable in this stupid heat.

I listen as The Colonel give the same speech he gave me and most likely gave John too. "Knowing how to survive in your environment is a forgotten skill. It's a test of who you are when only the cruelty of nature is watching. The animals out there do not care that you are a human being. You are just a source of food. Never let your guard down. If I hadn't, the tiger hunting me in the jungles of Vietnam would have eaten me. But I am a Kane, and I was faster. I killed that beast with nothing but my knife and my will to live. Now it is time for you to build your will to live with this test."

We all pile into The Colonel's truck for our three-hour trip to the women's Arizona State Prison Complex–Perryville in Goodyear, Arizona. It's the only women's prison in the state with a death row. My big brother gets the front seat because he's the tallest. I know I'm not done growing yet, and I want to pass him. On our way we take a road out into the empty desert where we drop off my little brother.

Mom kisses him on the cheek. "Be careful, honey." Then she puts a hat on him and gives him a bottle of sunscreen. "Find some shade. You don't want to get sunburned."

Austin wipes his cheek clean. "I will be fine. I'm tough enough." Then he salutes us.

The Colonel says, "We'll be back in three days. Remember what I taught you."

Then we leave. Mom doesn't cry this time. She cried when I did my survival test, but I was fine. Aside from the grasshoppers.

The rest of the drive, The Colonel talks about the importance of the death penalty and how it keeps society in check. I don't know if he's trying to convince us or himself.

During a pause in his rant, Mom changes the conversation. "So, John, have you told Victoria that you're back in town?"

John says, "Yeah, but she's been working a lot."

"Oh! She has a job. What's she doing?"

John pauses for a moment, thinking of what to say. "She's a…waitress."

"Really? Where at? We can all go visit her."

John refrains from turning around, avoiding meeting Mom's eyes. "I don't know. That might make her job harder, trying to spend time with us and working at the same time."

I say, "Why not? It could be fun."

John glares at me through the side mirror, silently telling me to shut up.

I smile back, "Don't you want to see her? Everyone loves seeing her."

I can see him grind his teeth as fire shoots from his eyes.

I say, "What was the place called again?"

He shakes his head "no," silently pleading again.

Dad takes one look at John, then says, "So she's stripping."

Mom looks almost as shocked as John, until we both start laughing.

John looks back and forth at everyone, absolutely dumbstruck. "Wha… How did…?"

Mom says, "Vicky has been talking to me since you enlisted. She wanted to be closer to us in case anything happened to you. She thought it would look good on a resume for show business."

"You freakin' knew?" John yells, his face red. He has to fight to not curse in front of Mom. "I knew Barry knew because he's so damn nosey, but both of you knew too?" He points to Mom and Dad.

The Colonel says, "No one told me." He shrugs. "It wasn't hard to figure out though. Why would you be so afraid for us to see her at work when you two text so much?"

John turns away, his face still red.

Mom says, "It's okay, honey. Don't be embarrassed. That's how your uncle met his second wife."

"I'm not embarrassed! And Uncle Rob's second wife is not a good comparison. Didn't she divorce him and leave him nothing?"

The Colonel says, "That would imply he had anything to take at that time."

We arrive at the large, dark gray prison complex on the western edge of the Phoenix metro area. I don't know why, but my first thoughts are of how I would escape this prison. Maybe I've been watching too much TV. I would start a riot and cause as much damage and chaos as possible, then disappear into South America. We park next to a beat-up sedan with chipped paint where a man with horrible burn scars covering the left side of his face calmy smokes a cigarette. His beard is trimmed short and doesn't fully spread across his entire face. His long hair is pulled back into a ponytail, revealing the stub that remains of his left ear. He uses his prosthetic hook hand to adjust his eyepatch, then uses one arm to pull himself up until he clicks his prosthetic leg into place.

I greet him first, trying to stay cheerful. "Hey, Uncle Rob!"

He drops his cigarette on the ground and stomps it out with his good leg. He never smokes in front of Mom for some reason. "Hey, kiddo! Don't I get a hug? Or are you too old for that now?"

I never liked giving him a hug, even when I was a kid. He always smelled bad, a mixture of cigarette smoke, various booze, and extreme body odor. But I go up and give him a hug because he probably needs one today. His grips me tight, crushing me against his beer belly. There's that smell. So much for my nice shirt. I look up at his scarred face. Napalm is one hell of a weapon.

He releases me when Dad walks up and says, "Good to see you, Will." He puts out his right hand to shake. They are a strange comparison, both covered in scars from their time in Vietnam, but Dad's scars are minor in comparison and he still has all his limbs, giving him a look of danger while his younger brother looks broken, disabled. Uncle Rob's head is only at Dad's chest. Both men are in uniform, Dad in his modern digital camouflage that he wears to work every day with an eagle and a shield to signify his rank, and Uncle Rob in his leftover greens that he has patched back together at least five times. One man is still proud to serve while the other can't let go.

A news van waits at the prison's entrance, which is not too surprising. My aunt is one of the most prolific serial killers in Arizona. She killed ten people to sell their homes for profit. From what I've learned, she would sneak into the house while the occupants slept and kill the families in their sleep, then clean out the house, hide the bodies in the desert, and sell the home to an unsuspecting fool. She was able to pull it off with three homes before they found the bodies in a burned up car out in the desert. Someone was bound to want to cover this event.

The Colonel steps in front of us as the news crew spring into action. "Excuse me, sir. Do you have anything to say about the execution of Rosemary Kane?"

The Colonel's eyes remain on the reporter with the microphone as the camera gets a good view of the long scars on his face from the tiger many years ago. "I have no comment for you vultures about the execution of my sister."

I guess they didn't see the name on his uniform.

Inside we have to confirm who we are with identification, which is the first time I've gotten to use my driver's license for something other than driving. Uncle Rob has to leave his hooked hand and prosthetic leg at the front because they say either could be used as a weapon, which is something I would like to see. A prison fight with a fake leg as the only weapon. I force my smile away before Dad turns around. I end up having to push Uncle Rob in a wheelchair through the compound.

Then Mom stops. "This is as far as I go. I told you I would come with you, Will, but I never said I would watch it with you. I have no need for that. I am a Kane in name only."

The Colonel nods his head with understanding, but Mom looks like she is on the verge of tears. How long has she been holding those back? I don't think she should be left alone right now. I look to John, but he has already turned away.

I say, "I'll stay here with you."

Relieved, she says, "Thank you, Barry."

But The Colonel's face lights up with rage. "No, you won't! You need to witness this! Don't you dare pussy out."

Mom says, "He's seventeen. Don't push him to do something he isn't ready to do."

The Colonel raises his voice just under a yell. "Don't baby him, Susan. He is a Kane! He will have to face this reality sooner or later." He turns to me. "Let's go! Now!"

I've never gone against anything Dad has told me to do before, but I stumble for words. "I…I think…I should…"

Then Uncle Rob reaches back to me and puts his hand on mine. "There ain't no stopping things now. We gotta see it through for Rosemary."

One word comes out as a cold acceptance. "Okay."

The few memories I have of my aunt are all positive. When we were in North Carolina, she flew out to celebrate Christmas with us and gave me a large Lego set. We went off the directions to make a cool spaceship with robot arms. She was arrested shortly after that.

The room is set up like a small theater. Several rows of folding chairs face the glass window of the execution room, which has a padded table with lots of straps and what look like doctors prepping a heart monitor. We sit in the front row. Several other people come in holding pictures of the loved ones they lost.

Dad says, "Don't look at them. Just keep your eyes forward."

I keep my focus on the window as two guards in full protective riot gear bring in Aunt Rosemary. She has handcuffs on both her wrists and ankles. Her hair is long and unkept. They struggle to strap her to the table, then give her a chance to address the audience.

She yells, "I regret nothing! You spinless cowards. I'll see you all in hell." Then she spits on the glass before the table is turned flat.

They clean her arm with rubbing alcohol and then insert a needle.

What is the point of preventing an infection during an execution?

A doctor injects something to put her to sleep. After thirty seconds, they give her a shot that slows down the beeps on the heart monitor. Then a final injection flatlines the machine.

A doctor says, "Time of death, 11:45 a.m., Thursday, April third, 2008."

CHAPTER 6

T HE DRIVE HOME IS QUIET. That whole experience at the prison felt wrong. It felt too clean. Shouldn't the end come with a fight before the eternal darkness? I refuse to go out like that. When I go, I don't want it to be sterilized. I want it to be memorable. As I bring the world down with me in my last stand against my enemy.

When we finally get home, all I want to do is watch some mindless TV for a while. Dad parks outside of the garage because there's not enough room in there for both cars and the home gym. When I get out of the car, I glance over at the smooth rocks that form a natural drain for water to prevent our property from flooding the few times it does rain around here. I don't know why, but it always catches my eye while walking to the door. Is it the different colored rocks or just how smooth everything is? It adds a nice contrast to our gray two-story house.

My brother's 1965 Mustang sitting in the driveway stands out in the neighborhood. Grandpa Joseph passed it to John when he died. His pride and joy, I think he loved it more than his wife. John has put every penny he has ever made into keeping that car alive. He just got it painted red with black stripes down the middle from the grille to the trunk. I asked to drive it once, and he laughed before cup-checking me as he said, "Over my dead body, twerp."

As Uncle Rob's beat-up sedan parks in front of our house, Mom says, "Why is he here?"

The Colonel replies, "He needs a place to stay for a few days."

Mom's head whips to Dad, and I swear I hear her neck crack. "What?"

"He doesn't have anywhere to go right now. He can stay in John's old room."

"Don't pull that 'he's your brother' on me again. Last time he stayed here, he wouldn't leave for months. I don't want him moving in just because he's been evicted from somewhere again."

Uncle Rob passes them entering the house with a small bag in his good hand. "Don't worry. I'll be gone in a few days. Your house has too many stairs for my liking. And I won't smoke inside this time." He flicks his used cigarette butt into the neighbor's yard, then follows me inside.

Mom and Dad bicker as I help Uncle Rob up the stairs one step at a time. His prosthetic starts above his knee, so he only has one leg with any strength. Our upward prog-ress is made more difficult by our golden retriever running up and down the stairs, excited to play with a new person. Rob stops to pet the dog. "Glad Butch is happy to see me." Before continuing his journey upward, he says to John, "You cool with me staying in your room?"

"Yeah, it's fine. I don't live here anymore. I'm just grabbing some things I don't want to get thrown out." He throws a bag of cloths into the hall. "I'm going to stay at my girlfriends for the rest of my leave."

Uncle Rob says, "Nice, but be careful about dating strippers. They'll take you for everything you own."

"How did you know my girlfriend is a stripper?" John grabs my shirt collar. "Did you tell him? You fucking snitch!"

I know this too well—fight back or get hit. I smack his hand away, immediately diving down for a tackle and ripping my pants at the knee. John sprawls out, dropping his weight on me and wrapping his arms around my chest as I keep reaching for his leg. John is taller and has Special Forces training, but I'm no pushover. I've been bulking up with weight training. Plus, we've wrestled dozens of times while growing up, so I know his moves. He'll try to get around me for a choke hold. As he makes his move, I trip him and roll us into the wall, making a loud thud.

Mom stops the argument with the Colonel to open the front door and yells in, "Bartholomew Kane, Johnathan Kane! No fighting in the house!" Then she closes the door again to continue the argument.

We separate, standing up quickly as if nothing happened.

Uncle Rob pokes John in the neck very gently with his good hand. "You're wearing a lot of glitter for someone fresh from deployment."

John rushes to the bathroom mirror in a panic. "Christ! It's everywhere! How did I not notice it?"

"Take it from someone with experience kid. That stuff doesn't wash off. It's practically a skin disease."

Mom and Dad come in after a few minutes, and Mom

is clearly not happy. She marches right up to Uncle Rob as he is laying on John's bed, reading one of my brother's many comic books, and she says, "You can stay here for *three* days. Then you have to leave."

Rob says, "I gotcha. I'm just sticking around till my nephew finishes his survival trial. Then I'll be in the wind."

Mom says, "Good. Now, please take a shower and wash your cloths. You absolutely stink."

Rob gives her a thumbs up. "You got it. I'll take a shower once John finishes."

I close my door to the usual chaos of the house and think about putting on some music. What I need right now is some Pink Floyd. Then I take out my math homework. Might as well get it done. If I try to watch TV right now, Mom will put me to work with more chores.

The next day, we get a call from Austin, who has apparently been picked up by the cops. They thought he was a runaway wandering the desert. Now my parents have to go retrieve him from the authorities and justify his training to the police. They both rush out to deal with this new crisis, leaving the house to Rob, John, and me. John wasn't able to go to his girlfriend's house last night because she had to work a double shift. Having already given up his bed to Uncle Rob, he chose the couch over Austin's tiny bed. I wake him up by turning the TV on super loud.

He grumbles, "You prick!" then throws a pillow at me, which misses me by a lot. He hasn't been able to hit me with a projectile in years. I'm too quick. "I'm still trying to catch up on sleep."

With a fresh bowl of Cocoa Puffs cereal in hand, I say, "Don't be so grumpy. It's Saturday, and they're doing an action movie marathon." I sit down on the couch, landing right on his feet.

He kicks free and rolls his head away from the TV. "Why bother? They edit out all the good stuff for daytime television. Plus, there will be more commercials than movie. It's easy to have a marathon when three movies take up the entire day."

After a bit of loud action movie explosions, John gives up on sleeping and goes to get some cereal as well.

I don't know why, but I feel compelled to ask, "John, don't you think it's ironic?"

He calls out from the kitchen, "In regard to what?"

"The execution, what else?"

He thinks for a moment. "It was clean and efficient. What else is there to think about?"

"Isn't it kind of ironic that both Dad and Uncle Rob have killed way more people?"

John eats his cereal at the table next to the living room. "It's war. There's a difference. Taking lives is the job."

"I'm just saying it's ironic."

John says, "That's why we serve. To use our family's curse for a just cause. Otherwise, we'll end up being put down like rabid dogs. I don't want to go out like that. I want to fight. You better still be planning on enlisting after high school. If you don't, you'll end up just like Aunt Rosemary."

I shrug. "Yeah, probably. I'm just not sure if it's actually a curse or an excuse."

"It is what it is," says the drunken gravelly voice from the back porch.

I nearly choke on the last bit of my cereal. Thank God it's soggy at this point. When the hell did Uncle Rob get downstairs? "How the hell are you so quiet with only one leg?"

"Years of practice, kid. There any more of that cereal left?"

John says, "Yeah, fresh box."

Uncle Rob appears in the kitchen and pours himself some Cocoa Puffs but uses whiskey and beer instead of milk.

John comments, "That can't taste good."

Rob says, "It ain't supposed to. Only point is to keep me drunk."

"How much you been drinking?"

He looks at John with an irritated look. "Enough to numb the fact that my little sister just got executed by the state. Enough to numb the constant physical pain I'm stuck with. So, I would say enough to knock me the fuck out and stay drunk for the next several days." Then he crushes the empty beer can against his forehead.

John puts up his hands. "Sorry I asked."

My phone buzzes with a text from my friend Nick. "Party tonight! You coming?"

Exactly what I need right now. Some fun with friends my age. A chance to cut loose. However, that might prove difficult. There is no way Dad will let me go out tonight after Austin just got picked up by the police. Dad will have the house on lockdown. Then there could be a second problem. If this is the normal kind of party Nick goes to, there will be booze and he only drinks to get wasted. I can't count on him to get me home and would rather not have to walk. But John doesn't live here.

I ask, "John, will you be spending the night at your girl-friend's place?"

John says, "Yeah…" His eyes narrow as he looks at me. "What are you up to?"

I have to keep my composure, can't let him know how much I need his help. "I might need a ride home tonight."

He smiles. "Sure thing, buddy."

That smile is definitely hiding malice. He says, "Twenty bucks."

"Come on, really? Uncle Rob, will you help me out?"

Uncle Rob says, "Sure thing. Forty bucks."

I should not have asked and just called them in the middle of the night. "John, you have a deal."

John says, "Easiest thirty bucks I'll make."

"Don't do that to me. The deal was twenty."

He nods. "It was, but I had to raise my price to keep up with my competitor."

I really need to get away from this family for the night.

Mom and Dad get home several hours later. They won't be facing charges for child abandonment as long as they take a long parenting class provided by the state for a hefty fee. Neither of them appears too happy. Not even Austin, who's probably angry about not finishing his test. And just as I predicted, Dad places the house on lock down. No one gets to leave for any reason, but somehow that only applies to Austin and me. Austin is more than happy to spend all his time going to school and staying home, but I want to go to a party. Dad's job has caused us to move from Marine base to Marine base. Is it really too much to ask to have a healthy social life at my school? No! It's not, and I see no reason for me to have to suffer the consequences of Austin failing his survival test.

Mom and Dad always go to bed at nine and are completely asleep by ten, so that's when I make my move. I can't risk going through the house because there are too many variables that could cause noise, but there is a reason that I chose the room in front, on top of the garage. I slip out through my window, onto the garage roof, and step carefully across the slippery shingles. I make my way to the edge of the roof, then place my legs over the side and lower myself down. Hanging from my hands, the drop is only about three feet. I land hard on my feet and freeze there to listen. Hearing the distant sound of a police siren, the hair on the back of my neck stands up. Have I been caught? I could scramble back up in one leap. Then the siren passes, and I take a deep breath. I need to calm down. This isn't the first time I've snuck out, and I've perfected my technique by this point.

I told Nick to pick me up a block from my house to avoid any possible sound waking my parents. I don't have to wait long for his light blue 1970s Volkswagen beetle to come speeding around the corner. It screeches to a stop just past me. I am so glad I didn't meet him in front of my house.

My friend hand rolls the window down and shouts over the loud music, "You ready to party?!"

"Born ready!"

We drive off, blasting music with the windows down. I feel free. Bad Religion comes on and we sing "Do What You Want" at the top our lungs. The song is short, so we start it over and sing it again.

Eventually we reach the party at a large house on the wealthy side of town. The house sits on top of a hill surrounded by other large homes. We have to park at the bottom of the hill, as dozens of other cars have taken all the closer spots already. I can hear music playing even from this far away. This is going to be a good night.

I ask Nick, "Whose party is this anyway?"

Nick says, "A friend of mine on the football team invited me."

"So, we weren't actually invited?"

He shrugs. "Sort of. It's an open invite as long as we provide something." He pulls out a bottle of whiskey with the security cap still on. I could protest the theft, but we'd get in more trouble admitting to the crime and, more importantly, I have no provable involvement. "Just play it cool, alright. No stoic tough guy routine. It's creepy."

"I don't do that. Do I?"

He almost laughs. "Are you kidding? You have a resting bitch face. Just be cool."

"Believe me, that's all I want to be tonight."

Nick reads between the lines. "Your dad still pushing you to join the Marines?"

Might as well be honest. He is my only real friend. "Yeah, and I really don't want to be directly under my dad's control anymore. But if I don't enlist, I'll be ostracized from the family entirely."

"Then join a different branch, like the army. I've heard Ranger School is as tough as it gets. You would be enlisted and have a level of training above your dad."

I like that, a way to both appease my family as well as get a leg up on them.

We arrive at an open front door where we see a bunch of people from our high school drinking and cheering for people playing beer pong. We are welcomed in by who I believe to be the host. There's probably about eighty people celebrating something. We weave through the crowd to reach the kitchen, where people hand us Jell-O shots.

"Cheers!" I slurp it down.

Nick stays to do more shots. As I predicted, he does not plan on going home tonight. I follow people into the backyard, finding the source of the music to be an amateur DJ, probably a fellow classmate. The pool is full of people swimming in either their underwear or street cloths. I grab a beer from a cooler. It tastes nasty, but I proceed to get a nice buzz going. It feels good to mingle with people, just leave all the bullshit behind for a bit. I start talking to a girl I recognize from my math class. I think her name is Sarah.

She's a bit tipsy when she says, "You want to get high? I heard they're smoking on the upstairs porch."

"You know what, I do."

There's a set of spiral stairs outside that lead to a small group of people chilling and passing a pipe around. I sit on a wicker couch next to Sarah and some dude who looks like he's fighting back tears, like he's one comment from a total breakdown. He packs a fresh pipe for me.

"Thanks, man." I don't want to say more. I am not going to be the one to trigger him.

He says, "It's fresh, got it dropped off earlier today."

I let out the smoke, feeling my body relax. "That's some good shit." Then I begin to cough uncontrollably as I pass the pipe to Sarah.

Before she takes a hit from the pipe, she says, "Are you doing alright, Pete?"

No don't ask?!

He shakes his head. "No..." Tears flow from his eyes.

"My little brother has a brain tumor." He tries to wipe them away as he continues to weep.

Sarah reaches over me, pats him on the head. "I'm sorry to hear that."

He keeps crying. "The worst part is that I can't even see him now that he's in Juvie."

Well, that killed my buzz. I came here to get away from all the morbid drama, but here it is again. I shouldn't leave the poor guy to well in his pity. Might as well make him feel less alone. "I get it man, shit is fucked up. The state just executed my aunt. Let's not focus on the bad stuff. Let's just get as high as we can."

Everyone looks at me with dumbfounded confusion.

His crying slows down, and he sniffles a bit. "Why was your aunt executed?"

"She was a fucking serial killer." I pass the pipe from Sarah back to Pete. "Like I said, shits fucked up, but let's try to have a good time tonight."

He takes a hit from his pipe, holds the smoke and then lets it out. With a slight cough, he says, "Thanks, man."

I didn't fix anything.

The pipe is reloaded and passed around. Pete is trying to come to grips with his losses. I pretend to listen to him talk as my mind drifts away. He keeps saying his brother's name, Jason. My heart starts to match the beat of the music downstairs, as I stare upward at the open sky. The one nice thing about the hot, cloudless skies in this desert are the stars. We are so small, so insignificant. The stars have watched us all this time. I wonder what the first Kane thought when he looked up to the stars all those centuries ago in the early days of Rome. After his first kill, when he murdered his own family for power, was he happy with the deal? Was he happy with the curse? Dad always kept the story deliberately vague, just saying it was for power. Grandpa said it was most likely a political move for wealth, but Great Grandpa Jack said it was a deal with the devil. "To kill one's own brother to guarantee his own line of succession. The family has been cursed to be killers ever since." That was probably the only story he ever told me before he died in 2000 at 100 years old.

Will I live that long? Do I *want* to live that long?

The party's getting rowdy. There's yelling and glass breaking. We all look over the side to see what's happening. Nick is getting pushed around by two attackers. One forces my friend to the ground and then the other kicks him hard in the side.

I rush down the stairs as fast as I can, then at full speed, I push one of Nick's attackers away. He loses his balance, falling to the ground seven feet away. I grab the other attacker by the back of his shirt collar and yank him away. He falls hard onto the tile floor.

I yell at Nick, "What the hell did you do?"

Nick rubs his side. "Nothing. I didn't know that was his girlfriend."

There's no time for anything more as the guy I first pushed comes back swinging a bottle at me. With no time to block, I am hit. The force almost knocks me down as glass shatters against my arm, dowsing me with liquid, but I plant my feet and grit my teeth. Without hesitation, I punch him square in the throat. He gasps for breath. Then I swing wide, hitting him in the left ear. He's shaken, and I press forward with a kick to his groin. As he bends over and grabs his hurt manhood, I connect an uppercut to his jaw. His body starts to fall, and my only thought is to finish it with another strike to the throat with all my weight behind the strike, but I'm blindsided by a force that picks me up and carries me away.

I didn't finish the primary target fast enough. He slams me into the gate leading to the pool. My back screams in pain, but I can take it. We struggle on the ground until I break free. We both stand, squaring up. He's big but not bigger than John, and I have fought with my brother far too many times to be afraid. Dad trained me to fight, not spare, to finish things, and I can tell by how he holds up his fists that he's got no real experience behind him.

The music stops as everyone circles us, no one daring to interfere. Phones are out recording what is to come. I take a step toward him, ready to strike.

Then we hear a bottle shatter on the ground as someone yells, "Cops! Scatter!"

My opponent drops his fists and runs. It takes me more than a second to process. If I get caught here, The Colonel will kill me. I make a break for it, jumping the wall around the house in a single leap. I see several cop cars blocking off the hill around the house, so I run down the side of the hill, going through waist-deep dry brush. I feel something sharp catch my calf, but it does not slow me down. I look around for Nick's car. "He's gone! I fuckin' knew it!" More flashing lights are coming up the street, and I see several people running into a nearby wash. I follow but slowly fall behind as the pain in my back starts to swell and my calf throbs with the same sharp pain. Looking down, I see a large piece of cactus stuck to the back of my leg and pull it out, but I get several small needles in my fingers that are too small to get out in the dark. I start running again. All my adrenaline is gone, but I can't stop. I have to keep going.

Eventually, I hit a road more in the city and try to call Nick on my cell phone, but he doesn't answer. He probably left his phone at the party or broke it in the scuffle. Either way, I can't rely on him to get me home. Good thing I thought ahead. I call up John, but my call goes to voicemail.

"Come on, you bastard. Pick up. We had a deal!" I try again with the same result. "Damn it!" He's probably getting busy with Victoria. How the hell am I going to get home? I'm miles away. There is no way I can make it back before sunrise by walking.

I wipe the sweat from my head, finding blood and glass tangled in my hair. Crap, how much damage did that bottle do? I start walking in the direction of home, thinking I should call Uncle Rob, he's my best option now. But there is a really good chance that he won't answer either. As his phone rings, I hear another phone ringing not far from me.

At a glance, I see a familiar beat-up sedan parked in the middle of an empty parking lot for a mini mall. "No freakin' way." Leaned up against his car is Uncle Rob with an empty bottle of booze in his hand, and he's snoring loudly with his head propped against the tire.

I walk over and kick his good leg. "Wake up, Robert." Then I jump back, ready for his inevitable response.

Rob's eyes open and his body tenses for a fight. He sees a silhouette in the dark parking lot and throws his empty bottle at the possible assailant.

I dodge it. "Calm down, you drunk. I'm your nephew!"

It takes him a moment before he lowers his guard.

"Shit…sorry, kid. You should know better than to wake a veteran like that."

I know all too well. "I need a ride home and anything you have to clean a wound."

He struggles to his foot, refusing my help. "Yeah, I got you." He takes out a fresh fifth of vodka from his passenger seat, pours it onto a wad of napkins he's taken from different restaurants, then hands me the soaking wet wad before drinking the rest of the bottle.

"Thanks." I wipe my face, feeling the burn of many small cuts on my face, but I don't feel anything too serious. I might be able to hide this from The Colonel? "Rob, what are you doing out here?"

He looks up to the dark sky. "Enjoying the stars."

I look up at the dark clouds. "I'll drive. You enjoy the stars."

He looks at the empty bottle of vodka. Slurring his words, he replies, "Probably a good idea."

Rob's car reeks of body odor, cigarettes, booze, and old food. There's a half-eaten can of Spam on the dashboard. I have to roll the windows down manually to get some kind of breathable air. I expect Rob to just fall back asleep, but he keeps looking at me with his one good eye.

Eventually he says, "Did I ever tell you how I lost my leg?"

Focusing on the road, I say, "From napalm, right?"

He shakes his head. "No, it was gone long before I got splashed with that shit. I lost it in the tunnel."

Talking to Uncle Rob usually only happens during holidays. He never really talks about his time in the war. "How did you lose your leg in a tunnel?"

He takes out a cigarette. "I was a tunnel rat, clearing the underground camps the Cong hid in during the day."

"Why would you want to do that?"

He tries to light his cigarette, but the wind from the car door keeps blowing out his lighter, until we stop at a red light. "I was fucking bored. The first four months of my deployment, we never saw the enemy. We just walked through the jungle, slept in the rain, and got bitten by bugs. We lost six people to punji traps. Then a sniper nailed our commanding officer. I didn't even get a chance to fire my weapon until I volunteered to go into a tunnel."

"Why the heck would you *volunteer* to go into a tunnel? Let alone one full of combatants? I thought you were claustrophobic." He freaked out one Christmas when he got locked in the bathroom and broke down the door to escape.

He takes a long drag from his cigarette, then blows it out. "I wasn't until after the war. It used to be easy to crawl headfirst into small spaces." He took another long drag before he says, "Honestly, I did it because of your father."

"What? But you two didn't serve together."

"Yeah, but I felt cheated out of my glory. Remember, I got to grew up hearing the legendary stories directly from Jack Kane. My favorites were the gun fights he had with the mob in Chicago and the stories of my father's exploits in both the second world war and the Korean War. My grandfather and father lived such amazing lives that I wanted my own war stories. Then my older brother goes to fight and comes back with a silver star from saving his platoon from an ambush. He even got cool scars from a goddamn tiger attack and wears the claws like a fucking medal. I wanted a real story so bad that I joined the Marines just like him and dove headfirst into seventy-six tunnels."

He looks back out the window, letting the wind blow back his long, greasy hair. I keep taking my eyes off the road to look at him. Having to swerve to fix my driving, I think I'm still buzzed. Thankfully, there's no one else on the road this late.

"I was good at it too. One of the benefits to being short. Until I lost my leg…" He stops as the memory boils back to the surface.

I say, "Not from the napalm," to show I'm still listening.

He shakes his head. "No, my leg was destroyed before that shit hit." He takes another drag from his cigarette before tossing it out the open window. "I swore that day I would never stay in a confined space again. That's why I always sleep outside, cold, rain, or heat. Even when your father lets me stay at his house." He looks off, lost in thought as he continues, "That's why she left me. I couldn't sleep inside with her. She could look past my deformity, but she needed me next to her and I couldn't give her that."

He pauses for a moment, looking like he's about to puke but just lets out a burp. "The last tunnel I went into was fresh. I knew because I had to crawl on my stomach for most of it. They hadn't gotten a chance to really dig out the tunnel yet. I was dreading having to shoot someone and drag the body all the way back out as I crawled deeper and deeper. There was a light coming up, and I was so focused on the possibility of finding people that I didn't see the tripwire. I was about five feet from reaching the first actual chamber when I felt several sharp spikes drop onto my left calf. It took everything I had to not scream in pain. I gritted my teeth so hard I broke a molar. But those sadistic fuckers also had another thing release with that trap. A jar of fucking centipedes dropped right in front of me. The goddamn things grow to be six inches long on average in Nam. I started fighting those fuckers with my hands, not wanting to alert any possible Cong in the room ahead, and they bit the crap out of me. They ain't deadly, but their venom hurts like hell. After killing them all, the reality of being stuck in the cave hit me. There was nothing I could do. The tunnel was too narrow to turn. Hell, it was so narrow I couldn't even take a full breath."

The streetlights give brief glimpses of his face. Is he crying?

"I was stuck there for at least an hour when I saw maybe a hundred fucking Cong file into the chamber in front of me. They were rushing to arms to fight my platoon." He takes a sip of vodka to clear his throat. "If they would have seen me, I would have been killed, but the Cong was preoccupied. They climbed out through a hole, right to the surface. I could hear the gun fight between them and my platoon. I was stuck between the enemy and dying in that tunnel. If I stayed, my platoon could call an airstrike that would collapse the tunnel. If my friends were all killed, then the Cong would find me and likely torture me to death."

"So, what did you do?"

He sighs. "I did the only thing I could. I took out my blade from my shoulder holster and put it in the ground." He mimics the action on the dashboard. "Then I pulled myself forward." He mimics the sound of tearing flesh. "I shredded my calf muscle off my leg." He doesn't look at me. "The will to live pushes you to do horrible things."

"Christ…"

His chokes down more booze before he continues. "That wasn't the worst of it. The only safe way out was back the way I came. I only had a revolver with about twelve extra bullets in my pockets. What was I going to do against a hundred enemy combatants with assault rifles when my hands barely worked from the centipede bits. I ain't no deadeye shot like Will. So, I pulled that trap out and proceeded to crawl back to friendly lines, with my leg oozing blood through a make-shift tourniquet. I was only in there for maybe two hours, but I thought I would be in there forever. I feared I would never get out.

"The problem was that when I finally did pull myself into the light of day, the napalm had been called danger-ously close. I would have been fine if I'd stayed in the tunnel a minute longer for cover, but I didn't and that shit splashed onto me. You're lucky they stopped using that shit. It's not just burning gas…it's more like glue. Got on my face, and I tried to pat it out with my left hand, only to have it burn as well. The napalm never even touched my leg. What re-mained of my hand and leg was amputated to prevent gan-grene from spreading." He looks longingly at the prosthetic replacement hook.

We stop at another red light, to no crossing traffic.

I finally ask, "Why are you telling me all this?"

Rob puts his hook on my shoulder. "Because I want you to understand that there ain't no glory for the second son. Don't hold yourself to his standards. I tried, and now, I'm literally half a man."

He has to stop to compose himself again, wiping the tears from his eye with his sleeve. "My grandfather was the son of the most feared outlaw in the Old West. Jack Kane ran away to France only to get pulled into the first world war. Grandpa Jack made sure his children and grandchildren knew the story of our family's legacy, and you will do the same for your children. That the first true Kane murdered his brother for power in the early days of Rome. Whether our family was cursed by the devil as a result, or he was just an evil man taking what he wanted does not matter to me. I stopped believing in destiny a long time ago. I believe the Kane family curse is a self-fulfilling prophesy we tell our decedents, then push them into dark directions. You are a Kane, but be your own man. Don't end up like me. I need you to promise me that!"

Promises are lies before the truth. "I…"

Rob slumps down, his head on my shoulder. Seeing that he's still breathing, I guess he finally blacked out.

I turn off the car's lights as I pull into my neighborhood. Slowly coming to a stop just up the street from my house, I park the car and Uncle Rob rolls out onto the ground, throws up a bit, then curls up on the sidewalk. He's on his side, so he won't choke on his vomit. Using a smelly jacket in his back seat, I give my uncle a blanket.

This was a dumb idea. I should have just stayed home. There's isn't much point in sneaking in when my face has too much evidence clearly displayed. I'm going to have several small scars on the side of my face now. Can't believe my bother abandoned me. He's probably making his limited time count with Victoria before he goes back to his unit. I have to bite the cactus thorns out of my fingers before I can lift myself back onto the garage and into my room. Thankfully, I left the window mostly open. Then I lay on the floor not caring to get into bed. In the dark room with nothing but the sound of my fan spinning above me, I still can't sleep. Tomorrow, Dad will make me regret sneaking out more than I already do. Not to mention whatever rumors will circulate in school from my fight. Hopefully they aren't too bad. I didn't lose, even though my only friend bailed on me.

Uncle Rob's words from our drive home echo in my head. Am I destined to kill? Maybe...

I do know I'll be eighteen before I graduate this year and will follow in my family's footsteps. I'll join the military like I am expected, but I don't want to join the Marines like Dad and John. I'm going to be better than them. I'm going to be a Ranger.

CHAPTER 7

MORNING OF CONSEQUENCES

MY HEAD THROBS FROM THE bottle impact. My legs are sore from running through the desert. My back burns from being tackled into a metal fence. I don't have the will power to get off the floor, so I begin to drift into sleep. I'll worry about showering after the sun rises. Then from the darkness, I hear the unmistakable voice of my father.

"Did you have a fun night, Barry?"

A pit opens up in my gut. I am so exhausted that I didn't notice my door is open. How long has he been standing there?

The lights flip on, the sudden brightness hurting my eyes. There stands William Kane in a pair of very short running shorts, revealing his hairy, muscular legs, and a shirt with the sleeves torn off, displaying his USMC tattoo in bold print on his toned bicep, above the deep scars on his forearms. Even in his late fifties, he keeps himself in fighting shape. He's never lost to any of his sons in any physical activity.

As he slowly sips a mug of what smells like fresh coffee, he says, "Was the party fun?" His voice sounds less than thrilled.

Oh shit, how did he find out? I thought I would have until morning to prepare, plus a shower to wash away the smells. I look at the clock in my room, seeing it's four in the morning. How am I going to talk my way out of this? "You see, I only went to study with some friends."

He enjoys a long sip before asking, "Did I not put the house on lock down after Austin got arrested?"

Does he smell the weed on me? I know he smells the booze. I was drenched in it. "Yes, but—"

"Glad you remember the orders." He takes long drink, finishing the mug. "Are you sorry?"

"Yes, of course." The party was not that fun.

He smiles. "Good. Now you have to prove it. I need all the large rocks from the front yard moved to the back. And if they are not done right, you will move them back and start over. Until I am tired." He takes two long steps into my room, his flip-flops slapping the floor. In one fluid motion he reaches down, grabs my upper arm, and lifts me to my feet. "Am I understood?"

"Yes, sir." I feel like absolute crap.

The sun rises two hours later as my whole body burns in agony. I empty the wheelbarrow full of heavy rocks in the backyard for the tenth time, leaving the front yard with only the dirt trench to drain rainwater, its colorful rocks now all piled up in the far corner of the backyard. I have to hold onto the wall to try not to collapse. The smell of food cooking inside reaches me. Mom must be up. I want food and sleep more than anything in the world right now.

The Colonel sits on the porch, watching me suffer. He scratches his chin where the long scar on his face ends. "What have you learned?"

Still trying to catch my breath, I wonder, *What* have *I learned?* I've learned not to get caught. Not to trust people, for they will abandon you when needed most. "I've learned I need to be better." I've decided I will never be a Marine. I will make my own destiny. I will become an Army Ranger.

The Colonel says, "Good. Reliability is how I earned my authority. Prove yourself to be able to accomplish every task you are given no matter how difficult. If I wasn't reliable, the Cong would have killed me and my team because sleep was more important. I have proven beyond a shadow of a doubt that I am reliable. Now you must do the same."

I let out an exhausted, "Yeah, sir."

Mom comes out onto the porch to refill Dad's coffee mug and says, "Glad you won't sneak out again. You're not as quiet on your feet as you think. Now, would you please put the rocks back in the front yard?"

They both chuckle as I begin to move the rocks once again.

I wish this wheelbarrow didn't have a flat tire.

CHAPTER 8

SOMETHING BETTER

"**Y**OU'RE A FUCKING RAT, ANGEL! Nothing but a backstabbing fucking rat!"

These are my father's final words to me as the bailiffs drag him from the court room. I should be happier, but all I feel is dread. He beat me and used me to sell his drugs. I owe him nothing. I do not regret testifying against him. I just wish I didn't have to. I want him to actually care about me, not use me. Why couldn't we go back to the way things used to be, before Mom and Dad split. I know things weren't perfect. They may have fought over every little thing every single day, but they were surely better than this.

I think to myself, *Don't cry, don't let him see that your hurt. You're a man now, and real men don't cry.*

My eyes feel wet. With each inhale, I feel as though it could all pore out.

No! I will not show any weakness. No matter how much I want to. The trial was brutal and took months for it all to play out. Mom couldn't leave Phoenix, but she sent me one postcard while I was staying at the Juvenile Court holding facility for the trial. It simply said:

> I'll see you soon.
> Love,
> Mom

It may have been short, but it was enough to give me hope while I had to live at the holding facility in the Juvenile court. There was nowhere else to keep me while all my wounds healed. Thankfully, I no longer need a sling for my arm, but my ribs took the longest to heal. I am very much ready to live in an actual home now.

I am being released into my mother's custody today. She was unable to attend the trial due to her work schedule, but the court arranged for a police officer to drive me the three hours from Yuma to Phoenix. Meaning more concrete, which means the heat sticks around longer.

I don't want to talk, so I just stare out the window from the backseat of the officer's cruiser.

The cop still tries. "Not bad weather right now. Normally, it would be getting hot, but the clouds have been providing some relief."

I don't answer.

He's looking at me through the rearview window. "It's a long drive from Yuma to Phoenix. It helps to talk about something."

I still don't answer. *I don't need your pity. It won't do me any good.*

"I've been doing this job for a while, and my favorite part is meeting all the different people I encounter. There was this one guy—"

I say, "I really don't care. I don't have the best track record with cops. I've been to Juvie twice, and the last time I got arrested, the drug dog nearly took my leg off." I point to the bite scars on my calf. "I just sent my own father to prison. I'll be seeing him in about ten to fifteen years. And my mother couldn't be bothered to come get me."

The cop stays upbeat. "That's rough, buddy. Like I said, I've been doing this for a long time, kid. There was this one time I was called to a car collision in a residential neighborhood involving a drunk driver. The car had crashed into a house at such a speed that the vehicle was completely inside the living room. When I arrived, there was nobody in the car. The only person around was the homeowner, drinking a beer in the kitchen. He said he just missed his garage. We had to get him to sign some paperwork to have his car towed, but he got defensive and tried to fight me and my partner. He ended up biting my arm." Points to the teeth-shaped scar on his forearm.

"Wait, he was already drunk and he was going for another beer?"

The cop says, "He didn't want to lose his buzz."

He proceeds to tell me about all the crazy stuff he had witnessed during his fifteen years on the force. He does not have a good opinion of opioid users. We eventually arrive at my mother's trailer park in the rough neighborhood of Alhambra, in northern Phoenix and pull up to a rusty yellow mobile home with an extended front porch. Car parts are littered everywhere. The wood porch creaks as we walk to the front door. There is no doorbell, so the cop knocks.

There is no answer.

I ask, "If there's no answer, will I get dropped off at detention again?"

"No, someone should be here." He checks his watch. "This was the time frame I was told someone would be home."

I would be disappointed, but I had no expectations to begin with. I guess that's just where I belong now.

A '90s era Volvo pulls into the carport. Out steps a Hispanic woman in khaki pants and a red shirt, her black hair pulled back into a bun. Her Target name tag is still on her collar.

I haven't seen my mother in a long time, and I know it's rude, but I think she's put on some weight since I last saw her.

"I'm here! Sorry, I got stuck at work." She grabs several plastic shopping bags from the passenger seat. There are dark bags under her eyes. With a smile, she says, "Hey, Angel, can you help me?"

"Sure, Mom." All these bags have blankets in them. She keeps all the bags that look like they have food.

The officer says, "Excuse me, but if you are Angel's mother, then I will need you to sign some paperwork before I can release him into you custody."

Mom says, "Yeah sure, bring it inside. I need to put this stuff in the fridge."

The cop holds the door open for us as we enter. The trailer is a bit of a mess, with clothes draped over the couch and the sink full of dirty dishes. When she sees the dishes, Mom mutters something under her breath along the lines of, "Damn it, Rosa."

The cop forces the paperwork on her before she finishes

putting stuff away. "If you don't mind, ma'am, so I can be out of your hair."

She puts away all the grocery's that need to be refrigerated, then takes the paperwork. She signs and dates several lines, then reads the last line to the cop. "I, Gloria Cortez Luna, hereby take my son, Angel Molina, into my care." She slaps the paperwork back into the cop's hands. "That work for you?"

The cop thanks her and gives her one of the forms for her records, then turns to me. "And you stay out of trouble." He winks and leaves.

I get that he was trying to be charming, but the wink was creepy. Like he expects me to get busted for something again. I have bigger plans than that. I have a notebook that's worth a fortune. I'll be on easy street in no time.

My mother and I are alone. "So…" I have no idea what to say. "What's up?"

Mom puts away the last of the groceries, then turns to me. She looks like she's ready to fall asleep as she walks over to me. She's only a few inches taller than me, but I brace for impact. Then she hugs me tighter than I think I've ever been hugged.

"I'm so sorry, Angel." Her voice is shaky, like she's crying. "I'm sorry I left you with Renato. I'm sorry I wasn't there any of the times you had to go to trial. I wish I had been. Every day I wished I could have been there, but…" She releases me from the hug but still holds my shoulders. "I'm glad you're home now. No matter what happens."

I don't know what to say. I resent her for leaving me with Dad, but I never expected an apology.

"Angel, I wish I could have had you live with me instead

of your father, but that wasn't possible. It's not because I didn't want you, but it was because I could not afford to take care of you. When your father and I separated, I had no job and all of his debt. I came to Phoenix for a fresh start and then I met Francisco. This is his home we live in. You will also meet his daughter Rosa when she gets home from school. She's a sweet girl, only a year younger than you. And you will have a new sibling in about three months." Mom holds her belly.

"Oh my god. I'm about to have two younger siblings!" I feel instant excitement, followed by fear. How do I act around them? How do you be an older sibling? Can I be a good example?

"I know this is a lot to take in, but there is something else I need to tell you." Mom looks sad.

"What's the catch?"

"We still can't afford you. Not with the baby on the way. With both mine and Francisco's jobs, we simply don't make enough. Thankfully though, Francisco talked to his boss at the restaurant and they will hire you to work in the back, off the record."

At least I'm not getting kicked out.

"Francisco's boss was also kind enough to help us with your room." She leads me down the hall and holds open a curtain door.

My room is a thin inflatable gray mattress and a dresser tightly packed next to each other in a space smaller than any cell I've ever stayed in. It looks like they just put one piece of dry wall over a closet and cut a hole in the wall, while the room next to it is untouched. Worst of all, I can't complain because the two other rooms are being used by my half siblings. I can't expect to share a room with my little sister, and the baby's room is all set up next to Mom and Francisco's room. I look at the room next mine to see a big bed with lots of space and full of girly toys. At least I get to sleep inside.

"Mom, what if I were to tell you that I have the means to make us a *lot* of money?" I take out the red notebook Jason gave me, noticing the front cover is starting to tear along the seam. "Within this notebook, there are mathematical formulas that I can sell to a scientist for a lot of money."

She flips through the pages, not taking the time to read them. "Honey, I never want to discourage you, but we need the money now. Not in eight months or even a few weeks." She hands the notebook back to me. "Keep studying. You have good penmanship."

"You didn't even read it. This is mathematical proof of parallel universes and how to reach them."

She's already walking back to the kitchen. "Honey, I've been working all day and my feet are killing me. I just want to sit down for a few minutes before I have to get dinner ready."

She doesn't believe me. Fine, I'll just have to prove it. I throw my only bag onto my new bed and watch the mattress deflate. Someday I will sleep on a real mattress with comfy pillows and soft sheets. I'll just have to make my way to a university on my own. It's not like I haven't ridden a public bus before. At least I won't have a backpack full of drugs this time. I can't get busted if I ain't dealing.

Dinner is an assortment of leftovers from the restaurant where Francisco works and discounted food from Mom's work. Mom mixed in some canned vegetables so we will eat healthy. We don't eat until Francisco arrives. A clean cut, tall, lanky dude, he looks like Renato's opposite.

"Hello, little dude. Your mother has said a lot about you," he says as he sits down to eat.

I can't imagine much. She's been away for almost seven years.

"I'll be taking you to the restaurant tomorrow after school. It's a good gig. You'll make better tips if you're clean cut. Might be time to shave off that peach fuzz on your lip."

"I've never shaved before."

Mom says, "Francisco will teach you. Right?"

Francisco nods. "Of course. It's not that hard."

When I get to meet my stepsister for the first time, her first words are, "Why is he living here now?"

Mom says, "Rosa, don't be rude. This is my son, Angel, and we will welcome him into this home with open arms."

Rosa looks angry at everything around her. "Is he the one that went to prison? Just stay out of my room, you criminal."

This doesn't feel like genuine hate. This feels more like a child trying to sound tough, and I've seen plenty of those. She has no idea what a tough person really sounds like. I could scare her, but what would be the point? "You have nothing I want. What would I do with stuffed animals? They don't have any street value."

She looks offended but not scared.

Francisco chuckles at that.

This will all take time to get used to. For the first time in a long time, I go to my own room with a door I can open and close at my will. With a full stomach, I lay down on my mattress. Sleep is unfortunately uncomfortable as I have to blow my mattress back up three times during the night. I hear the distant sounds of gunshots and police sirens about a mile away.

CHAPTER 9

A NEW LIFE

IT FEELS STRANGE BEING BACK at school. I don't feel free, just in a different kind of prison. I still have to ask to go to the bathroom. The school is surrounded by gates that are kept locked all day. At least the gates aren't topped with razor wire though. I could climb it if I had to. I do have the option to just not get on the school bus in the morning, but where else would I go? Not to mention, Rosa would rat me out if I ditched. She constantly avoids me when we are at school, yet she has no problem asking for my help with her math homework when I'm home.

It took them some time to figure out what grade I belong in. My math skills are far beyond anything they offer in junior high. While Juvie did have required school classes, not all the credits transferred over. I am placed in eighth grade with the expectation of making up all the assignments I missed in August and September.

My new baby brother Gabriel was born shortly after I started living with my mom. I know it's supposed to be a blessing, but he cries every night, waking up everyone. As if the combination of school and work isn't already wearing me down.

I have to do all my homework at school because there's no time after. I go straight from school to work my shift, not getting home until after ten. Exhausted from my shift, sleep will hit me like a brick and I don't even notice my air mattress deflating during the night anymore. The only thing that wakes me is my baby brother's crying every night. Mom can usually get him back to sleep. I just hate being woken up so much.

I had to write a three-page essay about *Hamlet* for my English class during my history class, then in my English class, I wrote a presentation about sharks for my science class, all in the same day. By some miracle, I'm passing all my classes but barely. I've stopped doing my math homework all together. The teacher never grades it and I ace all the tests. Besides all this math is simple shit—solve for X by dividing the answer. Jason advanced me far beyond mere algebra.

Honestly, the only enjoyable thing at school is basketball at lunchtime, and I'm good at it thanks to all the games while I was incarcerated. It's also the only place I feel like people don't look at me weirdly. I feel as if they all know I'm a delinquent.

I didn't help the situation by threatening an underclassman when I heard them making fun of Rosa for failing a test. The boy said to her, "How can you get less than half the questions right on a math test? You are so stupid you probably can't even add."

I'm not an imposing figure, so a show of strength wasn't going to work. I merely walked up behind the kid, uncapping my pen, then in a quick motion, I pulled his head back by the hair and held the pointed end to his throat. For all they knew, the pen tip was the edge of a knife. "Insult my sister again and it will end you." Then I softly whispered in his ear, "I've got no problem going back to prison for her." Which is honestly a lie. I ain't going back for no one. It was just the scariest thing I could come up with. The kid cried to a teacher, and I played it off as a Halloween prank. The teacher didn't buy it, and I got a week's suspension. They won't even look in Rosa's direction anymore out of fear of me. I now help Rosa through all of her math homework when I can.

One Saturday morning while I was mindlessly watching cartoons with Rosa, Francisco pulled me outside. "I need an extra pair of hands." He handed me a small wrench, then slid under his car. "I bought this Jeep fresh out of high school. Damn thing requires constant upkeep. Otherwise, it's dead in the water." He reached his hand up through the open hood. "Wrench, please. When I loosen this piece, I need you to hold it from your end or the other screws might bend."

I did as he said, helping him slowly take apart part of the engine to replace the timing belt before putting it back together. After starting the car to test the engine, Francisco said, "No matter how crazy my life gets, I know I can always fix this thing with my own hands."

I now look forward to working on the car with Francisco every weekend. I love working with my hands on mechanical stuff.

This is how I've spent the last year. School, work, and sleep. On the weekend, work, fix the car and help Rosa with homework, then sleep. It feels like too much sometimes, but that's just how it is. I'm able to power through most of my classes but fatigue always hits in my last class of the day. It doesn't help that the teacher sits in a chair in front of the entire class and speaks in a low, monotone voice. I'm so board, I can barely keep my eyes open.

I jolt awake as my desk shifts, returning me back to reality.

"School's over, Mister Angel. I'm sorry I bored you to sleep again," my teacher says in a sarcastic tone.

I franticly gather up my stuff. "Shit, sorry about that."

He stands at the edge of my desk, arms crossed, his glasses at the end of his nose making his eyes seem smaller than they really are. "Are my lectures not thrilling enough for you?"

"No, I just had a long night at work." Everything together, I make my way to the door.

My teacher stands in the way. "You seem to fall asleep in my class every week. You are going to have to choose between work"—he makes air quotes with his hands, like he doesn't believe I really have a job—"and your learning. Otherwise, you will not make it through high school."

Of all my classes, this is the one I care for the least. Fuck it, I'm going to tell him exactly how I feel. What's the point of lying? "I'm passing the class, aren't I? I advanced beyond this level of math a long time ago. I should be taking Trigonometry or Calculus, but this school requires that I take algebra because Juvie credits don't carry over. And regarding my work and future"—I mimic his movements exactly when I say future—"my mother just had a baby and my future is supporting my family. Now if you don't mind, I have to get to work."

I push past him. He's not fast enough to get in front of

me again. Tomorrow's class will be awkward, but fuck it, he was being a jerk. I'll fall asleep on purpose next time.

I see Francisco waiting in his clunker in the pickup lane and feel proud that our hard work is keep the old Jeep going. He's blasting heavy beats with all the windows down. Rosa takes the bus home while we go to work.

When he sees me, he shouts, " 'Sup, little man!"

I hop into the car. " 'Sup big man!"

"How was school? You get anyone's number yet?"

We have to yell over the music.

"You know I don't have a phone. You got to stop asking."

"Just trying to encourage you to talk to people. No need to be defensive. That's not going to help your chances."

"It's just hard. What if they say no and make fun of me?"

"Then they don't deserve to talk to you. And I'll let you in on a little secret." He turns off the music and leans toward me. "Everyone is afraid to ask."

"I call bullshit."

"Honest to God. By asking, you automatically become cooler than everyone else." Then he turns the music back up.

We arrive at the family-owned restaurant where I seem to spend most of my life, Mico's Place of Fine Mexican Dining. Francisco clocks in on the computer in the kitchen while I sign in on paper in the office. I'm still not officially employed since I'm only fourteen. I meet up with Baldeo to switch shifts. He's a Mexican man in his sixties. I've asked what his last name is, but he acts cheeky and says he's forgotten. He's already finished cleaning the washer space and is now assembling some kind of food concoction in the kitchen, a combination of ground beef, cheese, lettuce, and his special salsa.

"Angel! Come, come!" Baldeo passes me a plate full of food, all leftovers from the lunch crowd. "Enjoy! You must grow stronger."

I can always count on a meal here. I put on my plastic apron and go to the dishwasher as dirty plates begin to pile up. The job has gotten slightly easier in the past year now that I no longer need to stand on a box to reach the sink. I turn on the small radio just above the sink, balanced on an old pipe and the wall, to put my mind elsewhere.

Baldeo brings back the dirty plates and takes back the clean ones. I scrub all the dried cheese stuck to the plates with steel wool before putting them through the industrial dishwasher. Sweat and hot water splash everywhere. Hours pass as I clean dozens upon dozens of cheese encrusted plates. It feels like a complete waste of food. One customer only took a single bite of enchiladas before leaving. I have to scrape all this uneaten food into the trash. Such a damn waste. At least I have music to help me move to a beat.

I hear a song I like and reach to turn the radio up, but it comes loose, splashing into the full sink of soap and grime and shorting out. "Fuck!" The nasty water got in my eyes. My sleeves are wet. The cloth towels are gross, and I don't want them anywhere near my eyes. I have to find my way to the bathroom for a paper towel to wipe the soap out of my eyes. When I regain my vision and return to my station, I cringe at the sight of Baldeo bringing more dirty plates. "It never ends."

Baldeo says, "Cheer up. Only four hours to go."

Why is he always so cheerful? "Baldeo, how long have you been working here?"

He takes a moment to think, scratching his graying hair.

"Let's see, I'll be sixty-five soon, so…I would say twenty years now. It's definitely better than working the fields back home. I did that for twenty-five years."

"Where is back home?" He's never mentioned anything about where he is from before.

"Sonora, Mexico. I came here when I lost my farm. I haven't seen or talked to anyone back home in ages now. But no time to worry about that now. There is work to do." He taps on the pile of dirty dishes before returning to the kitchen.

With the radio completely dead, now all I have to keep me comfortable in the back of this old restaurant is the sounds of the high pressure sink interrupted by the roar of the dishwasher. I rebalance the radio on the same pipe as before. I ain't getting blamed for breaking the equipment. I am kind of surprised it hadn't fallen sooner. This place was built in the nineteen fifties, and I don't think anything has ever been upgraded.

Is this how I want to spend the rest of my life? Alone in the back of a restaurant, cleaning up other people's uneaten food. I haven't done anything interesting in the past freakin' year. Life was supposed to get better when I got away from my father, but all it has become is boring. It's been the same damn thing every damn day. I go to bed late, wake up tired, drone through the school day, then I come here. All my money goes to other people. I have nothing for me. I haven't made any real friends because I have no free time. I sacrifice all my time and have nothing to show for it.

I want more. I need more than this. I want to build stuff. I want to be challenged mentally and learn new things.

"God damn it, the damn thing is broken again!" rants the manager, Raúl.

What's broken now? I see Raúl in his white-collared shirt and blue clip on tie hitting the Salamander, a medium sized stainless steel broiler used to melt the cheese for nachos and other meals. This could be my chance to flex my mechanic skills.

I walk over and ask, "What's wrong with it this time?"

Raúl doesn't look at me as he smacks the oven again. "The damn thing won't heat up."

"Mind if I have a look?"

Raúl looks down at me, the light from his balding forehead reflecting in my eyes. "Do you know anything about fixing ovens?"

"Kind of…" Which is kind of true.

He waves his hand. "Then by all means. Tell me why it keeps breaking."

I could tell him that it's old and to replace the thing, but it needs to make it through the dinner rush. I can do a quick patch job, then maybe be promoted for my efforts.

With a quick examination of the oven, I notice the control dials are all loose. I need to look under the control panel to tighten things. "I think I see it. Git me a Phillips screwdriver."

I'm handed the tool. I take off the panel to see that the wires are disconnected from the loose dials. "I think this is the problem. The wiring is not connected. It needs to be re soldered, but I think I can hold it with tape and re tightening the screws."

It takes me less than five minutes before I close up the

oven. Okay, moment of truth. I turn on the oven. It heats up just fine.

Raúl says, "Good job, Angel. Now if you don't mind, the dishes are starting to pile up."

I look back to my dishwasher to see many stacks of dirty plates. Oh, come on! Couldn't someone have covered me while I was saving the oven?

I go back to work, cleaning the dirty plates like my handy work added nothing. "Ungrateful jerks."

Wait, what's that smell? Is something burning? I'm used to the variety of cooking smells, but this is making me cough. There's also a bunch of yelling in the kitchen. I look into the adjacent room to see flames bursting out of the cheese melting oven.

I let out a simple, "Oh shit." I already know what's wrong. The tape I used to fix the wiring was too old to hold and caused a short circuit.

I watch the flames spread to the nearby walls, then Baldeo shoves me back into the washroom as he franticly grabs the fire extinguisher off the wall. As he fights the flames, the air fills with a white dust that makes me cough even more. I have to walk out of the building to clear my lungs.

Oh shit! What am I going to do?

Due to the damage, the restaurant will be closed for extensive repairs. But this will no longer be my concern.

Raúl rushes out the door behind me and screams, "You little shit! I should have the cops drag you away for arson."

Thankfully, Francisco comes to my recuse. "Raúl, that's not going to help anything. I get that you're mad, but this was bound to happen at some point. All the machines are ancient. Your insurance will cover the damages. Just be thankful no one was seriously injured."

I say, "And you gave me permission to fix that thing."

Francisco stands in between us.

Raúl looks me dead in the eye. "Prey I never see you again." Then he goes to talk to the fire fighters as they finish putting out the fire.

CHAPTER 10

CHANGE

"**W**AKE UP, ANGEL!"

I shoot up, unsure of my surroundings. "Wha…" I blink my eyes, trying to focus.

"Perhaps you can explain the topic to class since sleep is so much more important."

I fell asleep in my math class again. What were we talking about? My notebook is closed, and I don't think even brought my textbook today. What's on the board? I see two equations in parentheses, each with an X plus a number. I say, "Just foil the equation, Mr. Lock."

Mr. Lock leans forward in his chair. "Why don't you show the class how it's done."

If he never gets out of his chair to teach, then why should I? Wait, this is because of what I said yesterday. He doesn't believe I should be in a higher math class, does he? "Fine then." I walk up to the front of the class.

With all their eyes on me, I feel nervous all of a sudden. Maybe I should have just stayed seated. Out of the corner of my eye, I see Mr. Lock sporting an arrogant smile.

I pick up a marker and begin drawing on the white board to show the work. "First, you multiply the first number in the sequence by the number two in the second set of parentheses, which will give you five X squared plus two X. Then you do the same for the second number in the sequence, which will give you three X minus ten. Add like symbols and you end up with five X squared plus seven X minus ten."

I toss the uncapped marker to Mr. Lock, who fumbles it and drops it to the ground. "Easy stuff," I say, turning to the class and expecting cheers, but I'm met with a complete lack of care.

I look at the clock above the board. Class ends in five minutes. They already learned this stuff and just want to go home. I quietly return to my seat and flip open my notebook.

Wait, I stopped taking notes in this class months ago. There was no point in copying math I already know by heart. This is Jason's notebook. This is the first I've looked at it since moving in with Mom. Jason put so much work into this thing. I feel an enormous amount of guilt that I haven't done anything with it since I was released. With my father's trial and then my work life, I've just been so busy, but no amount of excuses really justify my lack of trying.

I'll do something now. It's not too late. Jason said I had till 2012, so I'm still four years ahead of schedule. I just don't really know what to do with this stuff. I look back at Mr. Lock as he erases all the notes on the white board. I wonder if he would want to help me, being someone who likes math and all.

"Mr. Lock, I have some math I've been working on. Would you mind taking a look at it?"

He finishes cleaning the board. "Really? Is it at a level a mere mortal such as myself deserves to see?"

I turn to the first page. "I don't know. I just need a second opinion on it." Then I hand it to him.

He looks at the page, puzzled by all the writing. "What exactly is this supposed to be?"

"It's the mathematical steps to reach a parallel universe."

Mr. Lock's eyes light up as he starts flipping through the pages. "My God. How… How did you come up with this?"

I could tell him about Jason, how he's traveled to dozens of parallel worlds, seeing how it all happens first hand. I don't know how true all of it is. What I do know is that this could work. "It came to me in a dream, and I tried to figure it out." Not the best lie, but it should hold.

Mr. Lock reaches the last page. "This is incredible. Do you have any idea what you could do with this?" I hear him mumble under his breath, "This could be my ticket out of this shitty school."

I ask, "So I'm on the right track then? I'm honestly not sure what to do next."

Mr. Lock looks happy to a level I didn't know he was capable of. He's always so boring, so I was convinced he didn't have emotions. "Well, I do. May I borrow this notebook? I have a friend at the university I can show it to."

I snatch the book out of his hands. "No! This is my work. If you have someone to show it to, I want to meet them. This is *my* ticket out of here."

He stands frozen, holding nothing in front of him. His hands twitch. If he makes a move for the notebook, I will be ready to dodge. But he relaxes and replies, "I'll set up a meeting. It will either be after school or on the weekend."

I don't relax, but I say, "Thank you. I'll talk to my family."

I have to take the bus home for the first time in a while. Rosa pretends she doesn't know me, so I just look out the window and watch the city pass me by. We pass a small amusement park I've never been to. It looks like fun, but we could never afford it.

At home, Rosa hurries in to be alone in her room. I've never been home after school before. What do I do? I find Francisco working under his car and can hear faint cursing and the clicking of a rachet.

I lean down, " 'Sup big man. What's broken this time?"

He slides out, his hands blackened from grease. "Nothing anymore. Can you hand me a rag?"

The only thing remotely close to a rag is an old shirt with grease stains draped over the radiator. He wipes sweat from his face before he cleans off his hands, then turns the car on, checks the dials, and revs the engine before shutting it off. "Should hold together for a while. Would help if I could buy new parts rather than reusing slightly less broken old ones."

I ask, "Was it the transmission again?"

As we go inside, Francisco says, "Partly." Cleaning his hands in the sink with soap, he asks if I'm hungry.

I answer, "Yes, of course." The free lunch at school reminds me too much of food from Juvie.

Francisco stirs a steaming pot on the stove. The entire room smells of sulfur. "Well, I have some bad news. With the restaurant closed for the foreseeable future and with your mother working less to take care of your baby brother, my mother is going to try to help as best she can. She'll come by to look after you, Rosa, and Gabriel when your mother and I have to work. However, food is going to be more scarce." He grabs two bowls from a cabinet. "My morning construction job can only go so far. Your mother can get some food at a discount, but our budget is going to be tight." He pours the contents of the steaming pot into the two bowls. "So, I'm sorry to say, we are going to be having cabbage soup rather often."

He hands me the bowl with a spoon, then proceeds to eat his like it's a bowl of cereal.

"You're joking, right?"

He crunches the chunks of green in his teeth. "I wish I was. There is some baby food, but that's not for us. I'll see if I can get a night job, but it could still be a while. This is all we have right now."

This is my fault. If I hadn't tried to fix that oven... But I did. The guilt on Francisco's face tells me he wishes he could do more. He hates that he can't provide more for his family. He's not hiding food or anything, for that matter. He wouldn't be eating this soup with me if he was. I need to make this right. Now everything depends on Jason's equations.

I eat the soup, feeling full but not satisfied. A truly empty meal.

Mom is sleeping in a chair next to Gabriel's crib. I don't want to wake her, so I decide I'll tell them about the meeting with my teacher later. I go to my room and take out Jason's notebook. I need to have something to build with these equations. I'll have a better chance of selling the equations if they can actually make something.

My stomach growls at me. I am so hungry that it almost hurts, like there is a hole where my stomach should be. It's so hard to sleep on an empty stomach, so I spend most of the night trying to come up with design ideas.

Suddenly I am woken by a loud knocking on my wall. Rosa is the one with an alarm clock. I just wish she would be nicer about waking me. I look at the basic sketches in my book, finding I only have the start of one design. A sphere with emitters to create a portal. A typical flat portal won't work in a three dimensional world. The emitters will have to hit on the X, Y, and Z axes. I should check out some books from the school library for inspiration.

Now I have to figure out how to survive with no food and no income. I find the student doing the worst in Mr. Locks math class. "Five bucks, you can copy my homework. Ten for the test answers." That arrangement gets me through the school days.

Along with fresh cabbage soup, Mom buys cheap cans of soup and adds extra water to make each serving go further. This is not enough to live on, but it is all we have until Francisco can get another job.

Three days later, I go with my math teacher to meet his friend at Arizona State University. I have no idea what to expect, but maybe I can get a smeal out of this meeting.

It's a thirty minute drive from Alhambra to Tempe, during which time, Mr. Lock tells me about how smart his friend is and how hard he worked to become a physics professor. I hope he can actually help.

The university is pretty large. It's feels like a small city within the city. I wonder if it's hard to get into this school. We park in a tiny parking lot behind the science building. Mr. Lock then leads me to the largest classroom I have ever seen. There has to be over a hundred students gathered for this lecture. The notes are projected on the wall like a movie theater for science. The professor finishes his lecture and dismisses everyone.

I put my back to the wall as soon as the crowd starts moving. *Just breath. I'm not in prison anymore. I have no enemies here.*

Once all the students have left, Mr. Lock walks down to the professor. "Alan! It has been too long."

The professor turns back from resetting the projector notes. "James Lock, good to see you." They exchange a hardy handshake. "Glad you came. So where is this math genius you claim to have?"

Mr. Lock waves for me to come down. "This is Angel Molina."

I say, "Hi."

The professor shakes my hand with a tight grip that almost hurts. "Pleasure to me you, Angel. I'm Alan Knight."

Up close, I can see him better. He's wearing a sweater vest and a bow tie and thick glasses. He looks like a stereo typical nerd, but his grip was painfully strong. His long sleeves are partially rolled up, revealing toned muscles. This man hides his true strength.

"So, Angel, James tells me you have equations that prove the existence of parallel universes."

"Yes, sir, I do."

"No need for, sir. You can call me Alan. Can you show me what you've done?"

I hand him the red beat-up notebook.

He flips through it, clearly only skimming it. "Hmmm…I don't see any mistakes, but why don't you show me? On the old white board." Then he hands me a marker.

I knew I would have to do this. I have to explain someone else's math. What if I fuck up and they realize I'm a fraud?

No! I can do this.

Jason trusted me with this knowledge. He gave it to me to change the world. He taught me every aspect of his equations. I can do this. I have spent the past week reviewing this material. It's just another test, and I always ace the test.

Using a stool, I start writing at the top of the large whiteboard. "It all comes down to energy and distribution."

I begin writing out Jason's equations, slowly filling out the board. "It is possible to rip a hole in reality with enough energy. For example, every time we have fired off a nuclear bomb, we have created small rips in the space-time continuum. However, these rips do not last long after the initial explosion. And if anyone is within the ultra-heated blast area, they would be vaporized." Which is what happened to Jason. "In order to harness this power, the energy has to be generated without blowing up the city as well sustained indefinitely so we can access the rips."

I write the final bits of Jason's equations at the bottom of the board. "For every action, there is an equal and opposite reaction, so if we focus the exact same amount of power into itself to contain it, there is the possibility of a completely visible rip in time itself." I finish displaying the exact numbers needed to create the rip.

For the first time, I see all the equations stretch-out onto one suffice, revealing a new pattern. The letter C is used to represent the Constant, which is used many times in the equations and strangely forms an X shape across the board with the S for Singularity landing in the center. I wonder if Jason ever saw that.

I turn back to my audience, finding them both staring at the board with stunned expressions. Then Mr. Lock gently elbows Professor Knight, bringing him back to focus. "My God, kid. This is amazing." The words fall out of the professor's mouth.

Proud of my work, I simply say, "I know."

Professor Knight grabs some lose papers to write on. "I need to get this patented. There's so much we can do with this. I need to get to work immediately. I'll need to apply for a grant for funding."

With my hand, I erase a large chunk of the equation on the board. "What do you mean *I*? This is *my* work. I will be involved with anything that happens with it." I made a promise that I will change the world, not these two.

Professor Knight's face flashes with frustration for half a second.

I brace myself, ready to move.

Then he relaxes, knowing I hold all the cards. "You're right, I'm sorry. I got caught up in my excitement. *We* can do a lot with this knowledge. We need to patent this work so no one can steal it, but to do so, we need a copy of it fully written out. Now what is it you want to do with it?"

That is a good question. "I have a few ideas, but I haven't had time to really flesh them out. Can you give me access to the campus this coming summer? I think I can come up with a viable prototype in a month or two."

The two men exchange a look of intrigue before Professor Knight says, "Possibly, but what do you have in mind to build?"

Based on what Jason told me from his experience, I think I can recreate the link he had to his original timeline. "I think I can create a singularity as a doorway, or at the very least, a window into a parallel world."

They were not expecting that. I can see the slightest glimmer of fear on their faces before the professor says, "You do realize that a singularity is theoretically a blackhole? That could possibly destroy all life on this planet, right?"

"I do, that's why I need time to draw up the possible prototypes, make sure that doesn't happen."

Professor Knight puts his hand to his chin, silently thinking. Then he says, "I believe I can give you the access you need, as long as I am involved in the development."

"With free access to the cafeteria and a bus pass…if you can."

He smiles, "I can."

CHAPTER 11

ENDURANCE

"**I**S THAT THE BEST YOU got, Barry Kane?"

My eyes are heavy and my legs tremble. I have pushed my body to its limit, but I can't stop now. This is only the third day of Ranger School at Fort Benning, Georgia. The first day was full force takedowns and running with your partner carried on your back for hours. Then when the sun set, we ran to the obstacle course and crawled through cold, muddy water until three in the morning. It's so cold out I can see my breath. The second day, we had to swim in forty degree water. I'm from Yuma. Give me scorching heat any day over cold. Now, day three with no food and going nonstop for almost seventy hours, we march with sixty-five pound packs. People start to lag behind and I want to help, but there is nothing to be done. Staying back to help the weak will lower my own score, as well as drain what little energy I have left.

My battle buddy, Nick, is still right next to me, trudging along. At least I don't have to worry about him. I'm glad he enlisted with me after high school. Maybe he just felt bad about diching me at that party senior year, but either way, I'm glad he's stuck around. He may not have been the best partner for the grappling takedowns at the start though, since he is a head shorter than my six feet. It's hard to get takedowns on someone with a lower center of gravity.

We make it to the end of the ruck march in Georgia's dark, cold wilderness. The instructors order us to remove our packs and place them in front of us. I instantly feel lighter. Sixty-five pounds did not seem like a lot when I first put my pack on, but it got heavy real damn quick.

Cold, starving, wet, muddy, and bruised, my body begins to shiver uncontrollably. I think the current temperature is thirty degrees Fahrenheit. If I had any strength left, I would kill for warmth. I miss my long hair as my scalp starts to feel numb from the cold. Maybe this is the end of training finally.

Sergeant Clark yells, "Raise your packs above your heads!"

We all do it without hesitation. I lock my elbows to keep my arms straight. I am starting to hate Sergeant Clark. Short bastard should be kicked through a field goal.

Then Sergeant Clark says in a calm voice but still loud enough for everyone to hear, "We have been pushing all of you really hard for the past three days, so I'm going to cut all of you a deal."

The other instructors light a bonfire about ten yards away. The cold air cuts through my body. My teeth chatter. I do not want any attention right now, so I clench my mouth shut but can't keep the rest of my body from shaking.

"I'm sure all of you are hungry, tired, and cold."

I smell food cooking. *Do they have hot dogs?*

"We won't yell at you. We won't bother you in the slightest. Just quit now."

Mother fucker, that's just cruel! I can handle being pushed, but now you dangle the key comforts of warmth and food right in front of me. My arms tremble. Fuck, this pack is so goddamn heavy. This would be easier if I wasn't already exhausted. I hear a pack fall to the ground and see a candidate walk to the bonfire. A drill sergeant gives him a cooked hot dog as he warms himself by the fire. Then more packs drop to the ground. Now we know it's not a trick. They all look so comfortable.

My stomach growls at me. Shut up! You are not stronger than me! I'm going to be a Ranger damn it! I made such a big deal to The Colonel about not following him, I will make this work.

At least thirty-five people have given up out of the class of three-hundred-seventy. Thirty-five people sitting comfortably by the fire.

I will stand strong no matter what.

Then Nick slowly lowers his pack.

I whisper through my clenched jaw, "Don't you fucking dare!"

He doesn't look at me, his eyes fixed on the bonfire. "Sorry, Barry. This is your dream, not mine." He drops his pack, walks to the fire, and is given a freshly cooked hotdog. Sitting by the fire making jokes with all the other quitters.

After what feels like forever with our packs held high, Sergeant Clark addresses the remaining candidates. "You may put your packs down."

As we all drop our packs, I have to fight to keep from losing my balance.

Sergeant Clark says, "I want to now welcome all of you to the official start of Ranger School. We started with three-hundred-seventy candidates, and now we are down to two hundred. That is the average for the preliminaries. We expect to lose another hundred of you before the end. Only the best will earn the right to join the Rangers. Now clean yourselves off." He looks directly at me. "You look terrible."

He's probably right, but I know I will look worse before the end.

After showering off the many layers of mud and putting on a clean uniform, we're allowed into the cafeteria. We line up and are each given a tray of food and a spoon. Why is no one sitting at any of the tables? Then I see that the line goes directly out the other end of the cafeteria where a drill sergeant is having all uneaten food left on the tray thrown away. Cruel bastards. I have less than a minute to eat. I start shoving spoonfuls of meat and potatoes down my throat, almost choking as I force it down. Before I know it, I'm standing before the drill sergeant, who takes my tray from me and pours all my remaining food into the garbage. I don't think I've ever hated anyone on this planet more than Drill Sergeant Lee Clark. Several people quit on the spot.

Everyone loses weight in Ranger School. I thought that was because of the amount of exercise we get. Now I know it's because they just starve you. I'm six foot tall and a hundred-seventy pounds of muscle that I fear I'm going to lose here.

Over the next three weeks, we continue barely sleeping and barely eating as we move into the mountains of Camp Merrill to run combat simulations. I'm not used to the wilderness of mountains, but every military conflict has had some kind of mountain deployment. I will push through. While roping down a cliff in full combat gear, I slip. The rope catches me, but I now hang upside-down as my pack pulls me toward the ground far below. From above me, I hear several people laugh.

Assholes, would it kill you to help?

An instructor yells up to me, "Ain't no one going to save you, Kane. What are ya gonna do?"

I know, damn it. No one is ever going to help. I tighten my grip on the rope and fight the power of gravity as I try to stand sideways on a cliff side. I find a hold for my boot and force myself back into an upright position, then continue my descent down the cliff. I make my way through the rest of the mountain course, unlike a hundred other candidates who dropped out.

The final stage of Ranger School is simply called Florida. We will be airdropped into a swamp in the Florida Panhandle for sixteen days of simulated combat encounters. It strangely feels like coming home. I look around the plane at the remaining candidates, barely a third of what we started with. They all look tired, and some are even able to sleep through the sound of the plane's engines.

I have to yell just so the person next to me can hear. "This is the best part!"

Carter, a lieutenant who decided to become a Ranger after college, yells back, "I know. We're almost done."

"Not that. Florida! This is my old backyard!"

He yells back, "What?"

"I survived in the Florida swamp as a kid. This is going to be great!"

The red light comes on, and we get ready to jump.

I've been looking forward to this part. Despite how warn out my body is, I feel a sliver a joy to be home. I survived in a swamp outside of Tampa for three days with nothing but a knife and a water bottle. Having an M4 carbine and a backpack full of supplies would make this a cake walk for me.

The green light turns on, and we jump. I have no hesitation and feel no fear as I let gravity take me, my parachute string is pulled, and I float down. We land in an open field, pack up our parachutes, gather our gear, and head for the rally point. The mission is to attack an enemy base four miles away by following Lieutenant Carter's command.

The march slows to a crawl as soon as we have to pass through water. People get stuck in mud, their heavy pack's weighing them down. Everyone tries to avoid the water in the vain hope of staying dry, only to end up either stuck in more mud or wasting energy in harsher terrain. You can't fight nature. I stay in the water every time. I maybe wet, but I move faster than everyone else and keep ending up in front of the team.

Darkness falls as we reach the halfway point. One of the instructors relieves Lieutenant Carter of command. Trying to simulate the confusion of war, they'll probably place the lowest ranked person here in charge to shake things up. Wait, I'm a just a Private and I got promoted the day before Ranger School started. I am the lowest ranked person here.

"Private Barry Kane! Take point."

Well shit, guess it's do or die. It's only training. I won't die, but if I fail, I will have to restart Ranger School from the very beginning, which oddly feels worse. I've already lost so much weight that I don't think my body could handle that much trauma again.

I move to the front of the pack. "Alright, let's go!"

Everyone still moves slow. After sixty days of none stop training and very little food, I'm basically leading a pack of zombies.

"Stay in the water," I order. "All the snakes are on the shores."

Everyone jumps in the water. Men training to be on the best fighting force in the world are still afraid of snakes.

The water path bunches us up too much. If this were real, one artillery round would take out everyone, so I yell, "Spread out! We're almost there. This ain't even snake season. That's next month."

A lie. I have no idea when snake season is, but it works. We eventually arrive outside of the fortified base. I have to hit this place hard and maintain momentum. I'm not failing, not at this stage.

The fight starts, and everyone is still moving slow. Ten people pile behind one short wall.

I run up behind them. "What's the hold up?"

The one in front is shooting at nothing.

I yell, "It's clear! Move forward!"

He moves to the next obstacle.

Then I send another cadet after him, pushing them deeper into the compound. Where the hell are our light machine guns? I have to loop around the compound, where I find them also firing at nothing. "Reposition! We need suppressive fire over there!" I point closer to the objective.

Someone yells, "There's a man down!"

I run back into the compound, grabbing someone to

help with the man down. "Pull him back into the tree line!" I order two men who were barely focused to be of any use, just as the last room is cleared.

Done! We do a head count. Including the simulated injured, everyone is accounted for.

Sergeant Clark says, "Good job. You rallied and completed the mission. As long as you don't fuck up in the next ten days, you'll earn your Ranger tab."

That shouldn't be too hard…hopefully.

Then the day finally comes, and I stand among the remaining ninety-nine Rangers at graduation, feeling proud of my perseverance. Mom, Dad, John, and Austin are in the audience to see me receive my Ranger tab. It's black and yellow and not much bigger than my finger when they pin it to my uniform, but it brings me pride. It was the hardest experience of my life, so far at least. I feel lighter than I ever have.

Once the ceremony ends, Mom immediately runs up and hugs me. "I'm so proud of you, Barry." She squeezes me tight, then pulls back and holds me at arms' length, looking me up and down. "Have you not been eating?"

"That was part of the training. I've lost twenty-five pounds."

John jokes, "You didn't have five pounds to lose, shorty." He stands only an inch taller than me but has bulked up significantly from SEAL training.

As soon as I'm allowed off the base, I plan on spending some serious money on food.

The Colonel says, "Good job. Even if it ain't the Marine Corps." He straightens up and salutes me.

He wore his uniform to my ceremony. He sees me as

an equal now. I stand up straight, look my father dead in his eyes, puff out my chest, and I salute back. Mom takes a picture of this perfect moment. Then I look to my right and see both my brothers making stupid faces, completely ruining it.

I say with a smirk, "Really, guys?"

Little Austin just laughs.

John says, "Don't be such a sour puss. It's still quite the achievement. Now you should get one of these." He points to the Special Forces tab on his uniform. "You've already been through the physically grueling shit. This is the fun stuff. I even got to learn Arabic, *aint fasiq*."

"What did you just call me? I may not know the language, but I know when my big brother uses an insult."

He says, "Learn Arabic and you can figure it out for yourself, *aint fasiq*."

Better question, do I really want to do more training? This one kicked my ass as it is. No food, little to no sleep. I just want to deploy. I'm ready for some real action. But, then again, if I can survive this, I can survive anything. The next Special Forces Qualification course starts soon, and Sergeant Clark did mention there were spaces still available.

The Colonel says, "Don't be a pussy. Just do the extra step. It will be good for your career."

"Alright, alright!" I turn to John and Austin. "But when I graduate from that, you better not ruin the picture."

John says he won't, clearly crossing his fingers.

Austin says, "No promises."

I pull John aside. "Also, next time, do a better job cleaning off Victoria's glitter from your face."

He sighs. "I've tried. This is just a part of me now."

CHAPTER 12

WELL, THAT TOOK LONGER THAN expected, but now I have a Special Forces tab on my uniform. It took fourteen months of training just to find out John called me "a little punk" in Arabic. Not even an actual curse word. At least I learned how to hot wire a car during the evasion portion of the training. I'm also eligible for more unique opportunities and missions, plus the bragging rights that come with high tier training. I'll greet those as they come, but today I finally get to meet my unit before deployment.

The barracks at Fort Benning, Georgia are brand new. The army hasn't even finish painting it yet. Civilian painters are currently rolling on the white paint. It looks like an apartment complex. The first floor is essentially a large rec room with lots of open spaces, but I don't see anyone. The second and third floors are the living quarters. On the second floor, I find my room. It's basically a dorm, just big enough for two people. My roommate has the left side of the room, where he sits in a plastic chair playing video games on a small TV.

I say, "Hello, I'm PFC Barry Kane."

He doesn't look away from the screen. "Cool, call me Noob."

He has a California accent and terrible posture, looks like he's been in front of the TV too long.

"What are you playing?" Video games weren't something I got to play very much growing up.

He says, "Left four dead. I'm trying to get the gnome achievement on expert. Don't distract me." Then his character gets jumped on by a zombie in a hoodie. "Goddamn hunters! Come on team, help me."

My side of the room has a bed, a tiny closet, and a desk with a plastic chair. It's not much, but it will do. While I pack away my stuff, I hear yelling from the neighboring room. The walls are thin, but I can't quite understand what's happening. It sounds like they're moving out of their room and coming this way. Oh no, I didn't close the door. In walk four men in army green shirts and digital camo pants.

One of them says, "Welcome to the party, newbie!" Then he forces a six pack of beer into my hands.

I don't want to get shit faced on my first day. "Thanks, guys, but I'm not old enough to drink. Plus, what if the commanding officer finds out?"

One of the men with a thick black mustache says, "That would be me, Staff Sergeant Apone. Now don't be a bitch. We're drinking tonight."

I see another new recruit fresh from Ranger School trapped in a headlock by one of the drinkers. He's got the iconic large-framed, army-issued glasses, making his eyes look bigger than they are. He mumbles what sounds like, "I don't think we have a choice."

Still focused on his game, Noob says, "It's tradition, newbie."

In that case, I'm not going to look like a wimp. I take out my pocketknife and stab the bottom of one of the beer cans, then pop the top so I can drink it faster, shotgunning the beer.

Apone says, " 'Bout time we got a real warrior."

My first night with my unit, I drink more than I have ever drank before. I should pace myself, but I get caught up in the moment. I drink through the six pack, thinking the faster I finish it, the cooler I will look, but as soon as I finish, they give me more. The recruit with the big glasses drinks at a more reasonable pace. I hear his name is Burke.

I personally don't care for beer. Give me hard liquor any day over beer. I didn't grow up drinking soda, so I have no tolerance to carbonation, which makes drinking beer the equivalent of drinking acid piss. But, I refuse to look weak in front of these guys so I power through.

I learn the other two men's names are Hicks and Hudson, both from Texas. They look more and more the same as the night progresses. Hicks has brown hair while Hudson has black, and Hudson has a slight gap in his front teeth that he uses to whistle.

Staff Sergeant Apone is the one who pushes me to drink the most. He shows me a ring on his middle finger that has the words "Screw Love" carved in it and tells me, "Love is a lie. You think you have something special with someone, but as soon as you leave to fulfill your duties, the bitch will be banging Jody. Plus, she'll take the house, the car, and everything else you worked hard for." He chugs an entire beer before speaking again. "Only trust your rifle and beer. They will never lie to you."

I end the night hugging a toilet in the communal bathroom, puking my guts out until the world stops spinning and everything goes black. I wake up in the exact same spot, my body aching from sleeping on the tile. I shiver because the cold tile stole all my body heat. When I try to move, I feel disoriented, causing my stomach to jolt, which returns me to my previous position of puking into the toilet.

I hear a door open. "Newbie, you alive in here?"

I groan out the words, "I wish I wasn't."

A figure stands high above me and hands me a Gatorade bottle. "Here, you need to refill your electrolytes."

"Thanks." I take a big swig.

"Easy, drink it slowly or else you'll just puke it all up again."

I slow down my consumption, then try to stand. My legs feel wobbly, but the man catches me, helping my poor balance.

"Apone was impressed you actually kept up with them."

"Really? Then why aren't they in here dying with me?"

"Because they are professional drinkers. They drink every chance they get, and they're always looking for a new drinking buddy. Based on your current predicament, I would recommend against it."

My vision finally regains a more clear focus. "Who are you?"

"Bishop, the medic. It's a pleasure to meet you."

"Barry Kane. Likewise." I go to the sink to clean my face.

Bishop says, "Best get your stuff together. We have drills."

Our drills are designed to prepare us for combat as well as keep us in peak physical condition. However, my movement is slow. I want to puke, but I have nothing left. I see Hick and Hudson both keeping a healthy pace. How much do you have to drink to get an alcohol tolerance on that level?

"No daydreaming on the army's time, Kane!" Apone yells from behind me.

"Sorry, Staff Sergeant." I force myself to straighten up and instantly feel lightheaded. *Don't you dare fall. If they can drink and keep balance, then so can I, damn it!*

"Will you be joining us for more beverages tonight?"

I feel something boil up my throat at the mere thought, but I swallow it back down. "Yes, sir!" I am as tough as these guys, if not tougher. I can keep up.

"Glad you ain't a bitch."

That night, Apone pulls out the whiskey. I go shot for shot with everyone. More people join us. Drake and Frost are two actual giants. Drake is so pale he could almost be an albino with his white hair and blue eyes, yet I can't stop staring at the scar stretching from his left eye to his ear. Frost is the opposite in skin tone and doesn't have any distracting scars. They proceed to start a pull-up competition after we kill our two bottles of whiskey, and in my drunken stupor, I believe I can keep up.

The next day we go out to the tire pits for hand-to-hand combat training. Five-foot-deep holes in the ground are meant to be like a wrestling ring, but instead of a padded mat, the floor is saw dust and lined with old tires as wall padding. All the old rubber does is retain heat though. Just being near them makes me sweat. My arms hurt from doing too many pull-ups and my gut hurts from throwing up this morning.

Drake and Frost go first. The fight looks evenly matched, but Drake scrapes out a victory over Frost with a rear naked choke. Drake howls as we cheer for his victory. Burke is pushed in, and Drake throws the smaller man around like a ragdoll. Then Sergeant Apone points at me to go in.

This is my chance to prove my strength. When I jump in, the landing shakes me more than I would like and I instantly regret my decision.

Drake reaches for me as I dart in, wrapping my arms around his waist. I try to lift as he sinks down. He locks his large arms around my head. If I move my neck in the slightest, he will get under my chin and choke me. I reposition my legs around his and push, forcing him off balance, but as we fall, he lets go of my head and grabs my arm. He swings me to land underneath him. I try to brace my fall to no avail, quickly finding myself sandwiched between the ground and an attacker. Drake's elbow presses against my face, so I press my face against the ground as protection. I can't see anything, so I grab his arm and then kick out my legs. In one quick motion, I pull his arm toward me and wrap my legs around his head for a triangle lock. As I squeeze, choking him in between my legs, Drake taps out.

I let out my own battle cry, thinking the cheers are for me.

Then Hudson enters the ring. He smiles, showing off the gap in his front teeth. "Triangle lock not bad." He takes off his shirt, revealing a barbed wire tattoo around his collar with a skull and cross bones at the center of his chest. I take a wrestling stance as he approaches, my knees bent and arms up at the ready to grab. Hudson suddenly falls to side the and rolls on his back, grabbing my leg and twisting it in a way no leg should bend faster than I can blink. Turns out Hudson was a judo champion before joining the Rangers.

That night I drink to cope with the pain of losing. The left side of my back is badly bruised. I drink until I can fall asleep, only to be woken up, sore and still hungover for more drills. Strangely though, it feels like my left eye has something in it and then the next day it won't open. After four days, several strange circular bruises appear on my cheek and side. Why is none of this stuff healing?

I go to Bishop, who shakes his head. "You too?"

"What's that supposed to mean?"

He takes me to medical, where almost the entire platoon is waiting. "No one cleaned the pit, so everyone has ring worm from the pad."

"Please tell me I don't have a worm in my eye."

The medical staff take a look, "No, it's just pink eye."

The platoon is prescribed a cream to eliminate the ring worm infection, while I will also have to use eye drops for the next week. This shit better clear up before deployment.

CHAPTER 13

DEPLOYMENT

"T HIS IS WHAT YOU WANTED, Barry. You wanted to fight. To kill. Now take those butterflies in your stomach and direct them. I will surpass my brother and The Colonel in achievements." I mutter this to myself over and over on the C-17 aircraft flying me to the other side of the world.

We have shipped out to an undisclosed location in Afghanistan. When we arrive, I'm surprised to find that everyone on the base seems relaxed. Troops hanging out without any equipment nearby. Where is their sense of urgency for protection?

The barracks are small, but honestly, not as bad as I expected. Twenty-man tents with a green cot for each man.

Apone tells me, "Sleep with your boots in your bunk and shake them out every morning. Camel spiders like to sneak into them at night."

I say, "In Yuma, we had tarantulas that did the same thing."

Apone says, "Tarantulas are just creepy pets. The camel

spiders here are mean and their venom will rot away your flesh."

I don't take my boots off that night.

I expect we'll go on our first fire mission within a few days. A raid on a terrorist stronghold. Blackhawk helicopters will take us to a village with large walls far in the desert. Ropes will be thrown out, and we will slide down without a second of hesitation. The village walls will be blown open as we kick open doors and round up the villagers. It will be easy. I won't hesitate. I won't miss. I will kill all those in my path. We will suffer no loses as we are the best of the best. I will become what I want to be.

Unfortunately, things are slow. I should have known it would be like this. The United States has been in Afghanistan for almost a decade at this point. I was ten years old in 2001 when hijacked planes crashed into the World Trade Center, killing 2,996 people. Dad made me memorize that number. He said we would avenge every last one of them. I don't care about people I never met as long as I get to fight. I want the glory for finding and killing the lead al-Qaeda terrorist behind the attack. However, I feel as though few others share the same mentality today in 2010. All the passion for this war has dried out. Now we just pass the time.

This is Noob's fourth deployment, so he came prepared to fight the boredom. He smuggled in his Xbox gaming console as well as a two-inch black and white TV. He even convinced me to bring an extension cord, which he uses to steal power from the gas-powered generator on the officers building. Several other Rangers join in his gaming sessions.

Wierzbowski is a man of very few words. I honestly don't think he's spoken since I've joined the unit. Then there's

Crowe, who keeps bringing a helicopter pilot named Spunk-meyer to game with us. She always has her hair combed back and wears aviator sunglasses. At first it seemed weird that a female pilot would want to spend any time around rugged Rangers, but I think they have an unofficial relationship. She is the only one who can actually beat Noob at any of the games. I consistently lose almost every game I play, forcing me to give up the controller to the next contestant.

Over a week passes before we get a mission. A United States soldier has been captured by al-Qaeda insurgents. We are given a possible location and then deploy. Rules of engagement are to only fire if fired upon because this is a populated area, but I will not hesitate. I will kill all in my path.

We are given a very large location to search for him, a bombed-out town next to nowhere. Forming a strike team, we begin our search only to find abandoned buildings full of nothing, not even dead bodies. Anything of value was taken long ago. There's not even furniture left.

I enter the remains of a house with Drake and Hudson, slowly and deliberately, wary of potential booby traps. The Colonel told me how the Vietcong would put spike traps on just about anything back in Vietnam. I take each step slowly, with my M4 carbine ready.

I hear Drake's voice crack, "What the fuck!" followed up by furniture crashing.

I run to the nearby room with Hudson right behind me, ready for a fight. We find Drake with a chunk of rock raised above his head.

Hudson asks, "What the hell are you doing?"

With the rock still raised and his eyes fixed on the other

side of the room, he says, "I thought it was a small dog trapped under the rubble, but when I lifted it, I saw it was yellow with too many legs."

I say, "If it scared you, then why didn't you just shoot it?"

Drake says, "Fuck no! I ain't breaking the rules of engagement. Apone would end me."

The largest spider I have seen, over a foot long, scurries right at us. Its long, yellow hairy legs move so fast, it looks like it's floating. Drake throws the rock at it, completely missing. Hudson lets out a quick yell of fear. I freeze for a moment, not sure what to do. Trained soldiers afraid of a spider. I can't shoot it without getting my head ripped off by Sergeant Apone, so I jump high in the air, raising my knees up and then slamming my boots down just as it is under me. I feel it squish and rub my boots into the ground for good measure.

Drake says, "I fucking hate spiders. Leaving."

Hudson rapidly nods his head, eyes still wide, then follows him.

Was that my first kill in combat? A fucking spider. I feel cheated. I refuse to count that. I'm so focused on the bug, I don't notice the dog come up behind me. It bites my leg, shaking its head back and forth and knocking me off balance in all my combat gear. I fall, almost doing a split.

"Stupid Mutt!" I say, kicking at it with my other leg.

Its teeth rip through my tender calf muscle. Angered from the pain, I fire several rounds at the damn thing, blowing it apart. My leg is bleeding a bit, but it honestly doesn't look too bad, at least compared to the time my bike chain broke during a bad jump in middle school. Rusty thing cut me so deep I had to get twenty stitches. The whole squad bursts into the room guns drawn, only to find me getting up off the floor with a bloody leg.

Apone appears, looking ready to kill. "What happened?" I've never seen him this serious before.

"Fucking dog came out of nowhere, sir."

Apone violently shakes me by my combat vest strap. "Only fire when fired upon! I don't see a gun on that dog!"

I say nothing while wishing I had used my knife for the kill.

Bishop takes a long look at the dog before looking at my leg. With a look of fear, he says, "Apone, we need to get Barry back for immediate medical treatment."

"It's not that bad. Just bandage me up. I'm still good to go." I take a few steps back and forth with a very slight limp to prove my point.

Bishop says in a deadpan voice, "Look at the excess of foam around the dog's mouth. You just got bit by a rabid animal. You'll have to get the rabies vaccine."

Aunt Rosemary's execution comes to mind when I think of needles. *I will not show fear.* "I've had shots before. I'm not afraid of needles." I had to get a bunch before deployment and had a very slight reaction to the anthrax vaccine, which worries me a little.

We return to base without finding any evidence of the captured soldier. I am taken to medical and have to strip down to my underwear, which feels unnecessary considering it was on my leg. My wound is cleaned more thoroughly than it could be in the field. A series of shots are injected around the bite, which all burn real good.

Then the doctor takes out a syringe with a nearly five-inch long and overly thick needle. He says, "You'll need one of these every day for the next five days." Alcohol is rubbed on my stomach.

A primal fear kicks in. "Wait, wait, isn't this a bit archaic? Why not just more in the leg?"

The doctor fills the first syringe with liquid. "Maybe a bit, but the old method was thirty of these in the span of thirty days. Modern science has allowed us to only require five. I hear some places have made vaccines that no longer require stomach shots. However, we do not have those out in this desert. And having those expensive shots flown would cause us to miss the incubation time, resulting in you going crazy as the virus destroys your brain, then sending you into a coma and ultimately killing you."

I start to plead, "Can't you just call someone to check? We are the most advanced military in the world. I bet the modern shots are here somewhere."

Hicks says, "Don't be such a pansy."

I look over to see the entire squad watching my torment, and I flip my middle finger to them. I say, "Just get it over with," before griping the bed and hoping I can take the pain.

The needle goes into the center space between my abs, just above my bellybutton. When it pops through my flesh and then pierces my stomach, I tense up, trying to fight the pain. The needle feels closer to a knife wound. I can't breathe, it hurts so much. I can't scream, only let out a grunted moan of agony. When the needle is finally removed, I can only take shallow breaths as my gut hurts to move in any way.

The doctor smiles. "Good job. I'll see you tomorrow."

"I fucking hate you, Doc."

He merely applies a bandage of tape and gauze to the small hole in my gut, keeping his smile. "I know."

I have to slowly get up as the slightest twist of my stomach hurts beyond imagination.

Hicks and Hudson chant in deep voices, "Kane, the animal. Kane, the animal."

Back at the barracks, I lay on my back and stare up at the tan tent ceiling, my stomach aching with every breath. What the hell am I doing here? I'm not fighting. I'm just kind of suffering pointlessly. This is stupid. With no real point behind any of it anymore.

Wierzbowski comes by to give me a letter from home. He looks rather plain aside from the large mole on his cheek that I can never stop staring at. "Heard you got rabies shots."

That better not catch on. I take the letter from him with a very sarcastic, "Yeah. And I have another one tomorrow and the day after that."

"That's bad luck, Barry."

"Don't make that a thing."

"That's not how nicknames work." He continues to deliver letters to several others playing a game of Five Finger Fillet with pocketknives.

I tear the letter open.

Dear Barry,

It is important that you stay informed with everything. It is just as important that the enemy does not. Destroy this letter after reading. Your older brother is now among the most elite of Special Forces. With my guidance, he will have opportunities many can only wish for. You made it very clear when you enlisted that you did not want my help. However, I am here if

you ever need a push. One call from me and any problem
will disappear, I promise. Austin understands that too
as he prepares to enlist.

Sincerely,

Your Father

Did he seriously just send me a letter to brag about
John's achievements? I already knew he was a SEAL. I had
a phone call with John weeks ago. I crush the letter before
tossing it into the burn-pit can. *I don't need your help, old
man. I'll get glory on my own.*

While the rest of the squad gets to go on missions, I'm
stuck on post and forced to get a shot in the gut every day.
My days are filled with boredom as I have nothing to do
except for one moment of excruciating pain followed by a
painful several hours of laying around. A routine of monotony. Wake up, walk across the massive base to get chow—usually something with instant eggs, then get stabbed and lay in
bed until it doesn't hurt to move. All this silence makes me
ask, *Why am I here?*

When treatment ends, the nothing continues as we wait
for more unreliable intel. I return to gaming with Noob.
Currently he is absolutely destroying me in a fighting game.
Hudson whistles to us, the gap in his front teeth helping
him amplify it to a painful level.

I almost drop my controller. "Fuuuuck, is that really
necessary, man?"

Hudson says, "It is if it works. Anyway, gear up. We have
another possible location on that captured dude."

I say, "You know he has a name, right?"

"Yeah, but I can never remember it. Probably too many
head injuries."

Noob mumbles, "Or too much booze."

Hudson says, "Naw, probably not."

Noob and I look at each other, silently confirming our suspicions.

I say, "Alright, we're coming, but I swear if this is another empty house, I am going to have a long conversation with Intelligence that will end in bloodshed."

Hudson says, "I'm with you but only if it's their blood."

This time we come in on helicopters and fast rope down. I should learn this guy's name if I'm going to risk my life to find him. He was captured almost a year ago. What is the likelihood that he's even still alive? With the war winding down, there is little chance of finding him.

This time the place isn't empty. It's full of what looks like civilians, but that's the trouble with fighting an enemy that doesn't have a uniform. They could be anyone. We secure all possible threats as we move through our building. Other squads raid the neighboring ones, all of us checking for hidden rooms or compartments. We again find nothing.

"God damn it! Military Intelligence is absolutely useless!"

No one disagrees with me.

We release the frightened civilians and make our way out. Hudson is the last to leave our building. "Looks like you're going to have that bloody talk with Intel now?" he says with a knowing smile.

I turn back to confirm just as I see one of the civilians stab a steak knife into the side of Hudson's skull, just under his helmet. I don't hesitate. I lift my gun to end this threat. I see the smiling face of a teenage boy through my rifle's cross hairs.

Hudson is still standing and grabs the teen, hip tossing him to the ground. With his gun pointed at the boy, he says, "You little fucker!"

Dumb struck, I look for the right words, but all I can ask is, "Hudson, are you alright?"

"Of course I am! He only smacked me."

Holy shit, he doesn't know. Okay, I don't want to freak him out. Just remain calm and find Bishop. "Hudson, don't move. He hit you really hard."

"He must've. I can't hear anything out of my right ear."

Then someone says, "Sweet zombified Christ!"

I turn to see Hicks, Frost, and Crowe standing with absolute dumb expressions. I say as calmly as I can to them, "Someone get Bishop."

Crowe and Frost run off.

Hicks says, "How the hell are you alive?"

Hudson says, "It's not that bad, is it?"

As he goes to feel the damage on the side of his head, Hicks and I both yell, "Don't touch it!"

Hudson freezes. "Touch what?"

One of us has to tell him. I look at Hicks. "Do you want to tell him?"

"There's a fucking knife sticking out the side of your head."

Shit. I should have told him. We don't want him to panic.

All of us have to fight the urge to touch the blade until Bishop eventually comes rushing over, only to look more terrified than anyone else.

We gesture, not knowing what to do. Bishop takes

several long, unblinking moments to look at this incredible medical miracle, holding his hand over his open mouth.

He carefully puts out his hand. "Hudson, I need you to sit down so I can take a look at your wound."

Frost and Crowe secure the teen as a prisoner of war.

I ask, "Are you going to pull it out?"

Bishop looks at me as if I have said the dumbest thing he has ever heard. "No! I'm not a brain surgeon. My best guess is that the knife is currently *under* his brain. If we move it even the slightest amount, it could cut a major blood vessel. His best chance is for us to get him back to base as gently as possible and prevent anything, and I mean anything, from touching the knife."

He uses a Styrofoam cup full of gauze to wrap the knife after carefully removing Hudson's helmet, securing cup and all to his head. We chopper back to base. The entire time, I can't stop staring at Hudson and kind of want to take a picture. He seems so calm. Wait till someone gets a mirror.

None of the doctors at base want to touch the knife, so Hudson is shipped back to the States for brain surgery. I hope he makes it, but I doubt he'll return to active duty.

Already frustrated about not finding the captured soldier, now everyone is really ticked because they've lost a friend. Captain Weyland gets us a new detail, the general belief being that he believes the guy is dead and doesn't want the failure on his record. We are sent to the possible location of a bomb maker next. I'm not expecting anything. Whenever a high-ranking officer says the word "possible" with our rule of engagement being to fire only when fired upon, it means this will be a waste of time. Like everything else here.

When we arrive where there's an improvised explosive

device, others are sent off to search the surrounding buildings for the possible maker. The area has a decent amount of infrastructure. I always pictured Afghanistan to be desert with tan huts, but the roads are paved. The buildings are all the same color as the desert, but they are well constructed. There's even a five-story luxury hotel overlooking the block.

I rush over to where my squad mates are guarding the IED. I'd be lying if I said I didn't want to see it. As I reach them, everyone takes cover far away from me. "So where is it?" I say.

Hicks says, "At your feet, dumb ass."

I look down to see a pile of trash with wires sticking out of it. "That's it?" I was shown pictures in training, but this is just junk.

"Yes! There's enough power under there to take out the city block. Last thing we need is Bad Luck Barry to set it off."

I slowly back away, worried that my steps might set it off, then dive behind cover. "So what do we do now?"

Sergeant Apone orders us to form a perimeter and wait for the bomb squad to deactivate it.

Far from the bomb, I block off the street with Wierzbowski, Crowe, and Burke. As we wait for the bomb to be deactivated, I am simultaneously on edge as the bomb could go off or we could be attacked and unbelievably bored. If I knew there would be this much waiting for nothing, I don't think I would have joined. I want action, damn it!

Not much to do but talk.

"So, Burke, did the military issue you those glasses or are you just determined to remain a virgin?" Crowe says.

He says, "Very funny, but I'll have you know I am engaged."

I say, "You can't marry your own hand."

Wierzbowski says, "Probably can in Alabama."

"I'm not from Alabama. And I'm engaged to my high school sweetheart. I proposed at our graduation party."

Crowe says, "Careful with that. Apone did the same thing and now he's divorced and can't see his kids."

Burke says, "We're different. What about you and Spunkmeyer? Ain't that prohibited?"

Crow says, "Only if they are in direct line of command. She's a pilot. It don't get more separated than that."

Lucky bastard.

A young girl approaches our barricade clutching a stuffed animal.

I say in Arabic, "Go home. This area isn't safe," finally getting to use something I learned in Special Forces.

She says nothing and just points beyond us.

I repeat what I said, but she just stands there pointing. Burke approaches, waving her away.

Crowe yells, "Wait!" as he jumps to Burke.

Why do I smell glue?

There is no fire, just the force of the explosion. Dust, rocks, and the remains of both the girl and Burke fly outward. I'm knocked down, and the only thing I hear is a consistent loud ringing in my ears.

I shake my head, trying to focus. I have to remind myself there's a bomb maker in the area. *Get back to the mission.*

Burke is a mangled mess. Crowe clutches his neck as blood spurts out of his horrifically lacerated face. I rush over to do what I can and yell into my short range radio "Contact! We have two men down at the northwest interaction!" I can barely hear my own voice over the ringing.

"Wierzbowski, help me move Crowe into cover!" I doubt he can hear me, but he rushes to aid.

As the ringing fades, I hear the shot a large caliber rifle. Wierzbowski's face contorts as the bullet pierces his nose, exiting out the back of his skull. I raise my gun in the most likely direction of the shot and empty my entire thirty-round magazine, hitting every floor of a five-story building across the intersection. I slam in a new magazine before pulling Crowe to cover behind a building and then do what little I can in terms of first aid for him. His carotid artery has been severed, and I have to keep pressure on the opening. Then I feel another explosion rock me to my core as the IED we were protecting erupts into a large pillar of dust.

I keep the pressure on Crowe's throat, telling him, "Don't you dare die on me!"

Then Bishop arrives with a handful of the platoon and I yell, "There's a sniper over there!"

The platoon rushes off as Bishop kneels down to look at Crowe. He looks Crowe up and down before calmy saying, "Let go. He's dead."

"What…"

He lifts my bloody hands away. "There's nothing more you can do."

I lean back against the building I was using as cover. With one long look at my blood-drenched hands, I let out a defeated, "Fuck."

Sound slowly returns as I can hear the chaos in the nearby square. With this moment of clarity, a question arises. Why did the primary bomb go off? If it was on a timer, the bomb squad would have been able to disarm it. Both bombs had to be triggered remotely, most likely by a cell phone signal. The trigger man had to see how close we were to the kid. He wanted to do max damage, sending the signal as soon as he saw Crowe run to Burke, meaning the trigger man is also the sniper that killed Wierzbowski. He has to be where he can see both us at this intersection and the bomb plated down the road. The rest of the platoon has all the buildings guarded, preventing anyone from leaving.

I did shoot in the right direction! I broadcast into the radio, "He's in the building across the street." He's going to regret missing me.

I spring to my feet and run across the square, broadcasting into my radio, "I know where the shooter is! He's in the hotel."

Apone is already there barking orders at Drake, Hicks, and Noob to keep everyone in the building and the street clear. "Are you sure?"

"Yes, I am."

"Alright. I want that building secured. I want to know every single person here and why. Lock it down, Rangers."

The rest of the platoon comes to question people, slowly organizing the chaos. While I rush up the stairs, I think I hear Lieutenant Gorman try to stop me, but I'm too focused on finding the trigger man. He couldn't have been on the roof. It's too high up to get Wierzbowski through the nose. Every floor I run through to look out a window, none are high enough to see the second explosion. On the fifth floor, I hear a muffled yell of agony. I stop thinking as I run to the sound and then kick open the door.

A middle-aged man on the floor by a stove holds a red

hot knife, having just cauterized a bullet wound on his shoulder. His eyes dart to the room overlooking the balcony where an SVD sniper rifle sits on the floor next to a brick-like cell phone.

I can't help but smile as I carefully close the broken door. Then in Arabic I say, "You should have run when you had the chance."

He holds the knife out with one hand, not wanting to back down. I fire a single round into his right leg. He drops the knife to hold his bloody knee. I fire another round into his other leg, dropping him to the ground. Writhing on the ground, he yells curses at me that I don't know. Then I pick up the hot knife, feeling excited that my first kill will be this personal. This justified.

Before I am able to claim my prize, my arm is grabbed. "What the hell are you doing?" Hicks says with authority.

"Pay back! This fucker just killed a child and three of our friends."

"Christ, this is not the way, man."

More people enter the apartment. Hicks then stands between me and Lieutenant Gorman, blocking the view of the knife as the lieutenant enters with more troops.

Gorman sees the downed man and the rifle in the other room. "Good work. Get this man an evac. We'll need him to find the bomb maker."

The troops drag out the bleeding man as well as collect the sniper rifle, leaving me and Hicks alone in the room.

Hicks speaks before I say anything, "Shut the fuck up and listen. I know how you feel. This is not my first rodeo, and those aren't the first friends I've lost. But gutting a man will not bring them back or make you feel better. The bomb maker is still out there. Now, our only chance at finding him is that man. Otherwise, this shit will happen again. I'm glad you stopped him. The fact that he had a semiautomatic rifle means he was going to go on a shooting spree after the bombs went off."

"You didn't see a goddamn kid explode because of a bomb glued to her!"

"Don't lecture me on the cruelty of this war." His grip tightens on my arm. "I've had to pull the trigger on worse! I had to shoot a suicide bomber using a kid as a human shield." His eyes reflect the pain. "He was driving a car straight at our roadblock with a kid in the passenger seat, completely unaware of what was happening. The driver ignored all of our warnings. We did what we had to. All of us opened fired, and the car burst into flames, killing the driver and his hostage. I will carry that weight for the rest of my life." He snatches the knife out of my hand.

I didn't realize how loose my grip had become.

"If you had gutted him, you would have been court-martialed and then dishonorably discharged and thrown in prison. And the bomb maker would have convinced someone else to be the trigger man for another bomb." He drops the knife in the sink. "I didn't see the small bomb, but I saw the big explosion. The remains of the bomb disarming team have to be sent home in pieces."

He leaves me alone in that kitchen, blood on my hands from my friend and now blood on my boots from the trigger man. I should have just shot that man in the head. I kick a cabinet door in.

CHAPTER 14

FRUSTRATED

"**A**LRIGHT," I SAY TO THE camera. "This is Angel Luna Molina. At three in the afternoon on September third, 2010. First full-scale test for the worm hole." I wish I didn't look sleep deprived for this historic moment.

After over a year of constant work, to have finally reached a full-scale test run. I spent my entire summer almost living at the university physics lab, running simulation after simulation to develop this machine. Then I spent my freshmen year of high school going directly from school to building this device. Mom wouldn't let me drop out to pursue my destiny, so I've been operating on very little sleep and fueled by my new love of coffee. Professor Knight kept saying more would get done if I would simply leave my precious notebook with him, but I will not leave the answers to absolute power with anyone. They were entrusted to me and me alone. I only have two more years until Jason's prophesized apocalypse in 2012. All my work has culminated in this moment, the test that will change everything.

My machine is a large spherical cage of rebar welded together, thanks to Francisco. He needed work experience as a welder before the city would hire him, so it was beneficial for both of us. I have attached an energy emitter pointed straight at another emitter of the same energy. There are emitters of radiation, light, sound, and power, all to Jason's specifications. The idea is that with all these energies pointed at themselves, colliding in the center, we should be able to simulate the same amount of force that sent Jason through time and space. With a constant amount of energy flowing, we should see an actual portal open into another universe.

I retreat into a lead-lined room with my old math teacher, Mr. Lock, who refused to not be involved even though I have no idea what he does other than always looking over my shoulder to examine my work. Professor Knight preps the control panel. With this much power being funneled into one spot, it would be unwise to be able to turn it on with a single button. That would likely result in an overload of power.

I am very thankful for the professor's help. He has been the sponsor of this project, getting it green lit by the university and getting the money needed to fund this whole thing. Even though it wasn't enough, causing us to cut corners like using old machines instead of state-of-the-art technology. But it should be fine as long as the math still adds up correctly.

The machine slowly sparks to life and a small point of light begins forming in the center.

"It's working! Holy shit, it's working! I am the chosen one!"

But nothing more happens. It should be growing bigger as energy flows. Then sparks shoot from the control board.

"No!" we all yell in unison.

The board shorts out and the light fades. It wasn't enough. Why wasn't it enough? What went wrong? I will have to take the machine apart to find what went wrong. I was so damn close.

Jason said I would be the one to change the future and would do this with these formulas, but something is missing. Maybe I should ask him. If he's really from the future as he says, then he has to have the answers I need.

Professor Knight shrugs. "I guess it's back to the drawing board."

Mr. Lock nods his agreement.

They seem way too calm about this.

Mr. Lock says, "Angel, why don't you go home for the day. We'll clean up."

"No, I should try to figure out what went wrong. I'm too close to just walk away now."

Professor Knight insists, "Angel, you have been working yourself to the bone. You need to go home for some rest. You need a new perspective, because staying here another night will not help your state of mind. Trust me."

I don't trust many, but I suppose he has a point. "Alright, I'll catch you guys tomorrow." I pack up my stuff and leave.

I know where I have to go. Mom and Francisco will be working late. I can't rely on them for a ride. I've gotten used to riding the bus. It might smell like urine, but I can go anywhere I want. This time I need to go to Florence to see an old friend in Juvie.

After two hours and changing from a city bus to a gray

hound, I reach my destination in Florence. I am the only person to get off while one man covered in tattoos gets on. I walk to a large building surrounded by chain link fence and razor wire. This place is like home, and it feels wired to be here without being a delinquent. I almost walk up to the main entrance but quickly turn to the left for the visitor entrance, where I see none other than my corrections officer, Mr. Brook, talking to the receptionist at the front desk. He doesn't seem so tall anymore, though just as imposing.

"It's been a while, Mr. Brook."

"Angel Molina? Glad to see you're not in handcuffs this time. To what do we owe the visit?"

"I need to see Jason Baker."

His smile fades. "Oh…so you heard. I'm sorry."

"Sorry for what? Did he get into another fight? Let me guess, he's in solitary again. Not surprising. When will he get out?" I'll probably have to come by in a month. I should have called before coming.

Both Mr. Brook and the front desk lady look uneasy. Then Mr. Brook says, "Susan, please call Warden Fox down here."

In a matter of moments, Warden Fox walks into the lobby in his clean pressed suit and white hair. "Angel Molina, it's good to see you not in trouble for once."

Real original, dude.

"So, you're here to see young Jason Baker. Did one of your parents or guardians come to sign you in?"

Shit. "No, they're in the car."

Warden Fox thinks for a moment. "Normally you would need an adult with you, but considering the circumstances, I think we'll look the other way. Jason's time is running short."

"Really? I thought he still had another three to four years left before his release."

Warden Fox sighs. "I don't think he'll make it three more years, but miracles happen every day. I'm sure seeing you will bring him some light in this dark time."

I follow Warden Fox to the medical wing of the Juvenile Detention Center where we enter a room of medical equipment monitoring vitals. I see the completely bald head of Jason Baker sleeping. His cheeks are so thin that he looks more like a skeleton than the kid I remember.

I walk over to him. "Jason? What happened to you?"

Warden Fox whispers in my ear before leaving us alone, "It's a tumor in his head."

Jason stirs a bit, only opening his right eye. "Death has finally come for me." He tries to smile, but only the right side of his face reacts. He then tries to sit up.

I instinctively reach for him. "Easy, man. What's going on?"

He pushes away with such a weak effort, but I pretend that it worked. He says, "I don't need any help. Well, at least not yet. I still have some strength left, god damn it."

"What's happening to you?"

"Like I said, death has finally come for me. Unfortunately, she's taking her sweet fucking time, cutting me away piece by piece." He taps the side of his head. "Brain tumor. This timeline doesn't need me anymore. But these people won't let me die peacefully." He points to Warden Fox standing patiently just out of the room. "I have to live through my sentence. No matter how cruel the standard of life is. At least Luis will be protected when he gets here."

I ask, "Who's Luis?"

Jason says, "You won't get to meet him this time around. Shame too, because you two were such good friends. Listen, I appreciate you coming to see me, but there's nothing for you here anymore."

"Well, that's just it. I need your help. I'm having trouble with the formulas."

He looks at me with his one good eye. "I know you'll figure it out."

"I can't." I take out my notebook, showing him the results of my resent test. "I'm missing something. I can't create a nexus point like you showed me. How did you create your time rift?"

He says, "I didn't. I was next to a nuclear bomb that sent my mind back. All I know is that you will figure it out. Or at least, it will be figured out."

"What's that supposed to mean?"

He leans back down. "When I gave you the notebook of my formulas, I lost the connection to the nuke. Meaning that change set us down a new path away from the third world war. For all I know, someone you give that notebook to figures it out."

"Wait, you promised me that *I* would be the one to develop the new technology that changes the future. It's supposed to make *me* rich and famous."

"Angel, I don't know who really changes the future. I only know that it is changed. I don't have all the answers, just a collection of memories from dozens of lives. I've seen you die many times, but now it's all fading to black. I'm sorry I can't be more help. My only purpose now is to be here for Luis, and even that is becoming less and less likely."

Did he just use me? My eyes get watery. "You promised,

you said you believed in me. Am I not the chosen one? I betrayed my father because of you!"

He looks through me with his bloodshot eye. "You made that decision. I did not make it for you. Your father used you to sell drugs. You chose to have a better life. Now you have the opportunity to rise above all that."

He grabs my arm, and I can't help but think that his grip should not be this strong.

"Here's something from my many memories of the future. If you hadn't left him, you would have ended up back here in less than a week. Then you would have died brutally in a destroyed city on the other side of the planet. But more importantly, the beliefs of a dying man means nothing! Believe in yourself!" He relaxes. "Figure it out. I can't do anything for you now."

Warden Fox escorts me out of Juvie. We don't say anything until we reach the lobby.

I ask, "How long does he have left?"

Warden Fox replies, "We don't know, but we're obligated to try to keep him alive for the next four years. I doubt he'll make it that long. All we can do is make him comfortable. I hope you said your goodbye today."

"I didn't. I don't know how." Jason looked so weak, yet he was so angry. I came here for an easy answer. How the hell am I going to do this?

I get home before sundown for the first time in months. It looks the same as always. Broken car parts everywhere, it looks like Francisco was working on the drive shaft recently. I don't bother looking through the fridge, already knowing it's empty. I go to my room and sit on my deflated mattress. Not bothering to refill it, I just sit and stare at the wall. No real thoughts to a breakthrough come to me. I have no idea what to do. I've built a broken machine. Time is running out. I'm not the savior I thought I was. I am nothing and no one…no one at all.

Eventually someone comes home. As they walk by, I say, "Hi."

Mom jumps. "Jesus! Angel, you scared me. What are you doing sitting in the dark?"

"Nothing. Just nothing."

"Just nothing? Hmm…" She steps into the closet that is now my room and sits down next to me on the deflated air mattress. "Nothing sounds pretty good to me. Just worked a twelve hour shift on my feet."

So we sit there in silence for a bit until I finally say, "Mom, I don't know what I'm doing."

She kind of chuckles at that. "Welcome to the club."

"What?"

"Angel, I have no idea what each day is going to bring me, what new crisis will arise, but I still have to face it. Life is a constant mess." She stops for a moment, unsure if she wants to keep sharing. "Angel, I was one year older than you are now when your father knocked me up. I was seventeen and barely out of high school. I was scared, and Renato looked like he had all the answers. I thought I was a grown up, with my credit card building debt. When I realized how bad it had gotten, I ran and left you behind only to start another family with Francisco. I wanted to find you, but I was afraid of Renato. I spent many nights wishing I had taken you with me and now you hardly need me. You're self-sufficient. You're already working on something with the university I can barely understand."

I say, "It's just a doorway into a parallel world," as if I fully understand it.

"Exactly my point. Angel, it's okay to be confused and not know what you're doing. It makes you human. And it is only human to make mistakes. We couldn't afford you when first came back to me, but look at you now. You're still in high school, and you're building something out of science fiction. You even got Francisco welding experience and now he works for the city making more than he ever did waiting tables, plus medical insurance. You've accomplished too much to feel this sad. " She stands up. "Now, let's get out of this dark closet. Francisco is picking up your siblings and some chicken. We can have dinner as a family for once."

I ask, "Are you sure there's enough food for all of us?"

Mom turns back to me with a worried look that turns resolute. "Angel, we will have enough for everyone in this family even if they are smaller portions."

When Francisco finally gets home, he brings a big bucket of fried chicken in one arm and my baby brother in the other. It feels like I haven't seen them in forever. Gabriel already has a full head of hair that sticks straight up.

Rosa bursts in, excited for the chicken. Rather than giving me a look of disgust, she says, "Hey, Angel, can you help me set the table?"

"Yeah…sure." I don't remember where the plates and utensils are kept, so I just follow her lead. Then we sit down. I don't think I have any memories of eating dinner as a family before.

Rosa talks about school. She's having some trouble with algebra and asks for my help with homework. Francisco's current job with the city is welding bumps on park railings to keep kids from skating on them. It's rough, but the benefits are better than restaurant work. We all have a dentist appointment in two weeks. I don't think I've ever been to a dentist before. While Mom feeds Gabriel, she asks me to share what I've been doing at the university. Everyone stares at me with expecting looks.

"Well…it's kind of hard to explain."

Francisco says, "Just keep it simple. We'll try to keep up."

"I'm trying to create a doorway into a parallel world that exists in our past. But actual time travel is impossible. We can't change the past."

Mom says jokingly, "That's a bummer. Could make some investments."

"But we can travel to a parallel world where everything is exactly the same, existing at the time of our past. So, in theory, if there is an infinite number of parallels, we can travel to a parallel world that is existing in our present or even our future. I'm trying to create that doorway with the equations my—I mean, I created."

Francisco says, "That's pretty cool, little dude. Sounds like a lot of calculations."

"It is, but I've hit a wall. I can't get it to work."

Francisco says, "Maybe you're overthinking it. Maybe you need to look at it from another angle. By the sounds of it, you're focused primarily on time, but isn't time tied directly to space?"

Mom says with a hint of tease, "How do you know so much about time and space?"

Francisco shrugs. "I watched a special on TV not too long ago."

After dinner, I help Rosa with her homework at the table, but I'm preoccupied. I can't believe I overlooked space. Jason traveled through time to his younger self, but we travel through space constantly. I bet I could make a door to another point in space existing at the same time as us.

"Oh, Rosa, don't forget the minus sign. It changes the entire equation to a negative number."

Then the doorbell rings. Who the hell could that be at this hour?

Francisco opens the door. A man in a suit and a uniformed police officer are standing on the porch. Surprised but not scared, Francisco asks, "Can I help you gentlemen with something?"

The man in the suit asks in a deadpan tone, "Is Angel Molina here?"

What the hell do they want with me? I've been living clean.

Francisco says, "He is. I am one of his legal guardians. What happened?"

The man gives Francisco a sealed envelope. "He has been served as he is being charged with arson in relation to the restaurant known as Mico's Place burning down. All information is listed in the documents you have been given."

Francisco doesn't look at the envelope. "Is that all?"

The man says, "Yes," and leaves with the officer.

As Francisco closes the door, I say, "I was given permission to try to fix the oven under the boss's supervision. They can't do this."

Francisco says, "Quiet, Angel!" He looks serious for the first time. "We will deal with this, but never admit to anything when you're being served anything involving the law.

It will only make things worse, so shut up until we are clear of the cops."

With the door closed, we read the summons.

This is going to get way too complicated. I don't want to go back to Juvie.

CHAPTER 15

BACK TO THE HOUSE OF KANE

Fuck this place. There's so much work to do, but all of it is being blocked by many layers of bullshit. We can't do anything without approval from a superior, but they won't do anything without Military Intelligence confirming it. However, intel is almost always wrong because they need to go through multiple officers before it can be sent back to us and by then the situation has changed, leading to raids on empty or civilian homes. Deployment was supposed to be filled with action. My only kills were bugs and a rabid dog that took a chunk out of me. I watched three brothers in arms die from a distance. Four months of wait. Four wasted months with no real results. No wonder Uncle Rob chose to become a tunnel rat. If I was given the opportunity to do anything of worth I would have dove head first into a enemy filled hole.

The plane is quiet, I know I'm not the only one that feels this way. We didn't find the missing soldier. Now it's the next batch of Rangers job. It was someone else's job before us. I hate leaving a job unfinished. I also never got a confirmed kill. Every mission was completed without real combat. My only kill is that stupid rabid dog. I should have just shot that sniper in the head.

While back in the States I feel abnormally claustrophobic. I think I want to get a place off of base. I unpack my stuff but the barracks feel weird. As if nothing changed physically but something is missing. Noob just goes back to playing video games. I hate it when he gets melee kills, the sound is nothing like the real thing but it always puts me in the same head space of watching Hudson got stab.

The first night back Sgt. Apone physically drags me and Noob to a strip club.

"After every deployment this platoon gets a drink at the Foxy Lady. It's a good moral boost."

I say, "You do know I'm not twenty-one yet, right? I won't be allowed in."

Apone looks me dead in the eyes, "Kane, this is a titty bar next to a military base. They know exactly the clientele their getting. A bunch of lonely horny young soldiers looking to blow off steam. They don't check IDs."

After the platoon enters, everyone is handed a shot glass of whiskey. Apone says, "We drink together."

The thirty-two of us are the only clients tonight. Lieutenant Gorman stands up on stage, his big nose makes him sound nasally every time he speaks but he grabs our attention with three loud claps. "Welcome home, Rangers!"

We cheer.

"We raise our glasses to those who did not make it back."

We lift out glasses.

"To Carter Burke, Trevor Wierzbowski and Tip Crowe. May they rest in peace."

I was only one present for their deaths and I still feel like I could have done more. Shouldn't have hesitated on the trigger man. It is unfair he gets to live, even if he'll never walk again. Life is too good for him.

When we brought Crowes body back. Spunkmeyer broke down into tears. I haven't seen her since. There's a degree of separation from different units. I don't think I could look her in the eye.

Then Gorman gestures to the man entering the bar. "And to Bill Hudson. Welcome back."

Hudson lifts his glass up. A large bandage on the side of his skull as he tries to smiles but only half his face moves.

Noob mumbles, "I hate this part."

Gorman says, "To our brothers." As we all drink.

Noob coughs, "I hate alcohol." He switches to RC cola.

The music kicks in as the dancers come out for their routines. My eyes immediately focus on the ten bouncers peppered through the establishment.

I join the crowd around Hudson. He went in to surgery three months ago.

"The doctors say it was a bit of touch and go but I'm good now. Apparently the blade missed everything vital. The only real issue is that the right side of my face is pretty much paralyzed."

He peels off the bandage, revealing a two-inch long puffy scar along his temple. "Been wanting to take that thing off for a while."

Hicks ask, "So will you be joining us for the next deployment?"

He raises his beer, "Bet your ass I will. I am medically cleared and ready to rock."

Drake exclaims, "You are one badass mother fucker!"

"Damn right!"

Our attention gets pulled to the main stage dancer as she slowly strips away each article of clothing until she is in a skimpy bikini. She throws her top into the crow. Sgt. Apone catches it and we all cheer for him. He waves it around as if it were a flag.

By the time I'm on my fourth beer most everyone else is on their seventh or eighth. I've good buzz going. I need to speed up, I don't want to feel a thing tonight. Even if that means waking up on the bathroom floor again. I see Bishop and a bouncer helping the wasted troops to the door. Must be calling everyone a cab back.

Then Lieutenant Gorman and Sergeant Apone come up to me. Apone says, "Kane help me settle a bet. the Lieutenant. Can water catch on fire?"

Gorman says, "Water is H2O one part hydrogen and two parts oxygen. Hydrogen is flammable and fire needs oxygen to survive, so of course it can."

Apone argues, "No. Only what's on the water can catch on fire, like oil. That's why we use water to put out fires." He turns to me. "Kane, you're smart, right? Tell the lieutenant here he is clearly wrong."

I honestly can't give a good answer. Who ever said I was smart? "I dunno, doesn't water put out fire."

Gorman looks at me. "Damn it, Apone, you made another alcoholic in my platoon. Let's find Noob. If he hasn't left yet, he'll be sober enough to know the answer."

Apone takes a puff from his cigar, "Good idea." He playfully elbows me in the stomach gesturing his head to the dancers, "Keep up the good work Kane. You animal."

I straighten myself out. Put a stack of dollar bills on the stage enjoying my beer as the next dancer starts her routine. Around midnight Apone claims me as a teammate for a game of pool. They think I'm holding my liquor well but it's all an act, I am barely able to stay standing. Our opponents are Gorman and Bishop. Apone puts ten bucks on the table as a bet. I only have three bucks left. I think I spent too much on the dancers.

Gorman gets to break sinking two striped balls before missing. Apone goes next, he's still smoking the same cigar.

I have to ask, "How are you able to smoke a cigar for hours?"

He sinks a solid color into the corner pocket. "You don't smoke cigars kid. You savor the taste." He misses his next shot. "I became a cigar connoisseur after my divorce. Now I indulge myself with the finer things in life." He then blows out a smoke ring and takes a sip from a glass of scotch.

Gorman says, "That was before he grew his famous mustache. I might be the only one in the platoon to know what his face really looks like. He was a different man before the mustache."

Apone laughs, "I was a loser. Breaking my back to provide for someone who threw me away after my third deployment. The bitch had been banging some college intellectual."

Bishop takes his turn, "She's still the mother of your children. That has to account for something." He sinks one then misses his next shot.

Apone says, "Not to the courts. Apparently those are her kids and I don't get to see them."

I take my shot and immediately miss. I've never actually played pool before.

Apone carried us to a close game even though we end up losing. I only sank one ball. Well passed midnight I had spent well over three hundred dollars in single bills not to mention the charges from the ATM. Bishop helped me into a cab.

"Thanks buddy" I say, "You're a good dude."

It was the best I could do with my words by four in the morning.

Just to find Noob playing video games at peak volume. I mute his TV, which causes his character to die.

"Damn it!"

I say, "No words, need sleep." I fall onto my bed with a thud. As the sun begins to rise.

We are given a few weeks of freedom before we have to return to our post at Fort Benning. I take a plane back to Yuma. I didn't call because I wanted it to be a surprise. As I step off the plane I breath in the hot Arizona air. I should have gone to Florida. At least then I could have gone to the beach. It's a weekday, no one will be home. I'll make my grand appearance at dinner time.

I rent a car, drive to a Mexican restaurant. I been craving a real Mexican food since Ranger School. There is a severer decline in quality the farther north you go. When I get to the front of the line I immediately forget my order.

"Nick?"

It has been almost three years since I last saw him.

"Sup, man. See you made it through."

"Yeah… How've you been."

He looks exactly the same as he did in high school. Even the same haircut, I bet he would be wearing the same clothes if he didn't have to wear the restaurant's uniform.

"I've been good. Been working here, going to trade school. I'm going to be a plumber. They make more than teachers."

"Cool. What happened after you quit?"

He shrugs, "Not much, I was medically discharged. Turns out my legs were breaking. The X-ray looked like spider webs on my shins. So now I'm here. How was it? Did you kill anyone?"

I honestly don't know how to answer that. The honest truth is, "It wasn't what I was expecting."

I eat alone far from anyone. I cover my chicken enchiladas with spicy salsa. It burns with a flavor I had all but forgotten. I chug ice water to combat the heat. There was no ice overseas.

I drive around a bit not really sure what to do. I didn't grow up here, being here only for high school. Thus is the life of a military brat. I end up in the parking lot I found Uncle Rob almost four years ago. I even find a small pile of glass from a vodka bottle. There are a hand full of cars scattered here. I just kind of sit there for a long while. Letting the time really hit me. I'm almost twenty-one. What the hell am I doing? I'm a fighter that hasn't fought. A soldier that hasn't killed. I have an impressive title but nothing to show from it.

I finally decide to go to my parent's house. The place looks exactly the same. It's to be expected, I haven't been gone that long. I still have my house key. Upon opening the door Butch our golden retriever runs up to me excitedly barking. "Good to see you too buddy." To be fair you're happy to see anyone, you would greet a burglar exactly the same.

Austin is doing homework, a French workbook by the looks of it. Mom reads her own book. She has a pile of note cards to test his vocabulary. I remember her doing the same thing with me. Mom gives me a hug, happy to see I'm ok. While Austin only gives a quiet welcome back with his focus on his schoolwork. We don't talk about my deployment at all just stuff regarding their normal lives. I listen but I don't honestly care about Yuma gossip. Apparently Austin's classmate was diagnosed with a terminal brain tumor.

"The one that beat the crap out of five other kids and got arrested?"

Mom says, "Yes. I saw on the news that the family is fighting to get him out of prison. So he can spend the last days of his life with his family."

Austin looks up from his workbook. "He was kind of a quiet guy, until he cracked. The current rumor is that the tumor made him do it."

Eventually Dad comes home. He greats me with a handshake pulling outside, "We need to talk, alone." He grabs two Budweiser beers from the outside fridge, handing me one. I almost protest but he says, "Don't act like you don't know how to drink."

"Thanks, Dad."

We sit down at the table on the porch, looking into the yard as the sun begins to set. "Did you get what you wanted?" He asks not looking at me.

Again, I don't really know how to answer that. I didn't get my glory. I missed my chance to kill. My best friend couldn't cut it through training, quitting and abandoning me. I made new friends but three of them now are dead. I can't say no because then he will say I should have followed in the footsteps he laid out for me. So I say, "Sort of…" I shrug looking for the right words. "It definitely wasn't what I expected."

The Colonel keeps looking off into the Yuma desert.

"That's how it goes. When I joined I expected a fair fight in Vietnam. What I got was an enemy in civilian cloths using guerrilla tactics in an environment of hostile animals." He scratches at the scar on his face. "I got my glory during the Tet Offensive in '68. Was hardly a week into my first deployment when I was in a desperate fight for my life that resulted in the absolute destruction of our forward operating base. Everything's been an uphill climb since. I've been in the military for forty-two years now. I'm a god damn full bird Colonel, something my own father could never archive. I think I'll finally retire as soon as Austin finishes school." He looks to me. "I know how independent you want to be, but let me help you with your career. John took my help, got him the recognition he deserved. Just had to put his name in front of the right people, he did the rest. Now he's the captain of an elite Special Forces team, with nothing but upward to go."

I chug my beer to show how easy I can drink. Then place my empty bottle hard on the table. "I can do it on my own."

"I'm not saying you can't, but if you let me help, it'll go much faster. I have a meeting with an old friend can make anything happen. It will just be putting you on the right team."

I almost say no, but thinking of how little I was able to achieve. There is no real control out there just layers of bullshit. This is an opportunity to cut through all of that.

"Fine."

CHAPTER 16

'M GETTING TOO OLD FOR this. I turned sixty last month and I can feel my body slowing down. My knees don't bend very good anymore, while my back is in constant discomfort. I take a handful of pills every day and my doctor wants me to quit drinking coffee. Grandpa Jack told me to never grow old, yet he made it to a hundred. Dad said the same thing before his heart gave out, but Dad was never that healthy. I just thank god he didn't live to see his only daughter get executed by the state. I know my sons will never go down that path. I've raised them into fine military men. Susan wanted them to be less like me but they're Kane at the end of the day.

At least I can say I'm proud of them. Unlike my grandfather who killed his father in the Tombstone streets back in 1910. The curse of Kane takes its toll from each of us. It took away half my brother. I feel guilty every time I see him. I think he hates me, even though Robert would never say it. I honestly thought he was going to kill himself after Rosemary was executed, but he's still kicking his one leg somewhere in Vegas. They were very close. Shame it had to go down the way it did. The curse affects us all.

I need to help Barry get better opportunities. He is Special Forces but that doesn't guarantee he will get real action. In this current war many soldiers go their whole tour without killing. Thus is the problem with the tail end of a conflict. Everyone is tired and wants to get home in one piece. I'll make a call today after my meeting to a friend in the army. I'm sure I can find someone that owes me a favor.

I should focus considering what is coming. Normally our meeting would just be a phone call. I only ever see him in person if it's important. At his level everything is important. My office is clean, with everything where it needs to be.

My office phone rings. "Colonel Kane. His plane has landed, and he's heading your way."

"Thank you, Jackson."

I used to get nervous when he would visit. He would never be in a good mood, angry at the world. He's calmed down in the recent years. I think the fall of the Soviet Union helped with that.

In walks a bald man in a black suit. He closes the door behind him before taking off his sunglasses to reveal his blood red oval eyes. "Hello, William."

"Yabechun, what's the crisis this time?"

He smiles, "To the point. I always appreciated that about you." He takes out a small box from his jacket pocket.

My inner Marine comes out.

"Sorry, old friend. But I'm spoken for. Susan would not be happy if I left her for you."

He doesn't acknowledge my joke. He opens the box to reveal four General stars.

"You are not retiring."

My heart skips a beat. I am lost for words for the first time since John was born. There is no refusing him, but I was going to retire to spend my days taking cruise ships around the world with Susy. Eventually I find the words I need. "Why? The cold war has been over for years. You won, all that's left now is the small conflicts. Let some West Point kid have those fights."

He places the stars on my desk.

"Not for long. For what shall come will change the world, ideally for the better. I need real veterans to lead the fight." He turns to look out the window, gazing upon the airfield. "I know Jack told you many stories about the first world war, but he didn't spend much time in the trenches. Waiting in the wet mud until the shells stopped. Then we would charge through the barbed wire. All to get cut down by machinegun fire. As the tide strikes the shore, we would fall into the opposing trenches, ripping each other apart with spades. Only to retreat back to our trench when their reinforcements arrived. It wasn't the carnage that bothered me. No, it was how nothing was ever gained even after years. The leaders were all highly educated aristocrats with no real fighting experience. Sending waves of young men to their deaths, then blamed us for our lack of progress. They thought it was a good idea to charge a fortified enemy positions using automatic weapons on horseback."

He mimics a perfect noble British accent. "The Calvary will break through the lines."

His voice drops back to a somber tone. "Consider yourself lucky you will never know the smell of hundreds of rotting horses." He looks back to me. "The world has changed many times. Each time because of war. Rifles replacing warriors with soldiers. Chemical weapons kill a hundred men with one jar of yellow gas. Now the Atomic Age ending human freedom."

I want to add my point of view to his speech, but it's best to just let him go.

"War is a necessary part of the human experience for advancement. While maintaining a population that can lead through the toughest of times. The next great war will force a restructuring of our society. We can't keep using technology dependent on limited resources. Not if there's to many with not enough to go around. I'll need real combat veterans to lead the next war. All those who have moved up in ranks from the Afghanistan and Iranian conflicts will make good platoon leaders. But I need someone who fought in a large scale conflict to lead them. You won't underestimate your enemy and you know there are no real rules in war."

In Vietnam the idiot in charge during the Tet Offensive, spent the entire time hidden under his desk while we fought for their lives. Then claimed the victory as his own after doing nothing. A live grenade rolled into his bunk one night. No one saw a thing.

I take the stars. "How long until the war?"

"In two years I will have the blight that is North Korea wipe from the map. Then the world powers of China, Russia and the United States will battle for supremacy. The world will be reborn a new through fire. Prove to me this country is strong enough to lead the future."

Excitement fills me, "We are far more terrifying than those commies. We are well practiced in international war. When was the last time either of them actual had large scale conflict that wasn't against a bordering country? Russia lost to Afghanistan back in the 80s and China hasn't fought since they got destroyed by Japan in World War II. All our combat tested soldiers are still young enough to fight. When will the promotion be official?" When I tell Susan she's going to be pissed but I know she will understand in the end.

"Next week, the announcement will be made official. You'll be stationed in Washington DC. Once the war starts, your judgment will determine your location."

Now I can personally make sure my sons get the glory they deserve.

CHAPTER 17

ONLY THREE MONTHS FROM THE last deployment, we are shipped back overseas. I was less than a week off before I returned to training. I'm a Special Forces Ranger days off are few. Now the Company is being sent to an undisclosed location in Iraq. Surprised they didn't send us to aid in the pull out of Afghanistan. President Obama wants to have all troops out by the summer of 2011. Let's see if they can pull that off in the next in four months.

I don't feel nervous this time. But I have to tell myself that. I want to be here. I want choose to fight. Barry Kane will not go home empty-handed this time.

The tents in Iraq look exactly like the barracks in Afghanistan. Military construction has a universal look, gray concrete and efficiency. The only difference is the tent color, military green. I found a faded stamp dating the tarp back to 1950.

I wish I didn't have to sleep near Hudson. He snores so loud now that half his face doesn't move. Not that there ever is much sleep in a combat zone. We survive by taking short naps at every opportunity.

Then we are sent out for our standard mission of raids on possible of al-Qaeda terrorist cells. Majority are dry holes. One time we raid a family home. We account for everyone except the father. I find him in the back placing a metallic object in a large pile of rocks that used to be a wall. I point my rifle at him then yell, "Don't you fucking move, motherfucker!"

He freezes with an uncomfortable smile. "What is that?" He doesn't answer. I repeat the same thing in Arabic, to the same response. "Pick it up!" There's no way I'm touching a possible bomb. "I said pick it up asshole!"

Sergeant Apone and Hicks appear behind me. "He put something into the rocks. And is acting dumb."

Sergeant Apone says, "If he doesn't pick it up, we'll have to arrest him and call in a possible IED."

Fuck! I refuse to have a repeat of Afghanistan. In Arabic I yell, "Pick it up, you stupid punk, or I will kill you and your whole god damn family!"

He stops smiling at that and picks up the metal object. Turns out to be an old tin box of money. He was afraid we were going to rob him. Just a waste of fucking time.

The hardest part is always the fight against boredom. Noob's gaming system died in transport. When ever we turn it on the normal green lights turn red.

I join in the game of Five Finger Fillet. Hudson stabs the knife from the gap between his thumb and index finger then out to each finger gap at record speed.

"How do you do that?" I ask.

He wiggles his fingers to show a good amount of scars.

"Years of practice." Then blinks at me. As he passes me the knife.

I take the blade. "I don't think you know how to wink anymore." I begin trying to match is speed. I have to stay focused.

Apone yells, "Barry!"

I cut my ring finger just below the nail. Then hide my hand away pretend nothing happened. "Yes Sergeant?" Trying to look professional as I feel my finger sting.

"Mission for you. Looks like your Special Forces certification will actually be used this time. Report to the airfield as 1300" He hands me a envelope with all the info I need. "And clean up your hand before you embarrass yourself."

I'm flown to a forward operating base. All I'm told is to prepare for a full day hike. I'm so excited! Finally some real action. I find the commanding officer.

"I'm Specialist Barry Kane. Where's the staging area?"

He lets out a laugh then walks away. I guess that means this is the staging area. I prep all my gear. A hundred fifty rounds of ammunition for my M4. Plus an additional forty-five for my M9 Beretta. Enough water and rations to last me for a week in the desert. I have over prepared but I am ready for anything.

The team is of five people none of them tell me their names. All of them are in very casual get up. Bear minim gear, just basic day packs for hiking. Only two of them have rifles, another M4 and an SR-25 sniper rifle. These dudes must be really hardcore. We start walking into the desert.

I ask "What is the mission?" They ignore me, so I press, "I was requested for this. I need to at least know why in order to do my job correctly."

One of them says, "We have the location of a bomb maker. In a village a few mile north from here. And you're only here because someone above us put you on the mission. You must have a friend somewhere high up to get you this gig. You are not required."

So this is Dad helping my military career. A hike to kill a bomb maker. He's a goddamn General now, and I'm Special Forces. Couldn't he get me on something cooler. Like mission to kill a high-ranking terrorist protected by a small army. We would lose many in the battle but I would secure the target. Instead I'm on a hike with people who couldn't care less.

Someone mutters, "I bet you didn't even earn that tab."

That crossed the line, "Fuck you. I earned everything I have. Worked my ass through Ranger School and Special Forces, ain't fasiq."

He looks back at me, "You punk. Is the best insult you got?"

"No, I learned that one out of spite for my brother."

We reach the village after 20 hours of nonstop hiking. Someone makes a call on a radio. Within minutes an F-22 fires a series of missiles on the village, reducing it to nothing in seconds.

Someone says, "Target eliminated." Then they all start walking back.

I stand there for a moment watching the sands burn in the night. "What was the point of that?" Are humans even needed? That could have been done with a drone to confirm the location then the plane could have been sent.

Nearly three months into this deployment we actually

get a rock-solid location on a high-ranking al-Qaeda leader. We expect heavy resistance.

Holy shit this is real! Fucking A!

Our platoon is taking three Blackhawks as the tip of the spear, with Captain Weyland bringing the rest of the company in a transport helicopter. I prefer the Black Hawk design personally. The transport looks like a giant banana to me.

I end up in the center seat of my helicopter, the worst seat because I'll be the last one to get out. I would rather be the first to jump. I don't want to be sitting still when bullets start flying. Our team leader, Corporal Hicks, sits directly across from me. We'll jump at the same time. He's so calm, it's kind of off-putting. I keep tapping my leg in anticipation. Noob passes me a pack of gum. I take a piece then pass it to Hicks but he doesn't move. I gently kick his leg, he jolts into focus. The son of a bitch had been sleeping for the entire helicopter ride. He takes a piece of gum and passes the pack to Bishop.

I yell, "How the hell can you sleep before a combat drop?"

I think he yells back, "What?" It's impossible to hear much of anything in a helicopter.

We descend close enough to the ground to release the ropes. Bullets plinking our ride as the rope drops. This is when the fun begins.

Hudson and Drake slide down and Bishop follows. An explosion from the helicopter's tail rocks us and we begin to spin. I grab my seat for dear life.

I feel the seat belt, no time to think, and I click it around my waist. I pull the strap over my left shoulder but I can't find the strap for my other shoulder. My body feels like a ragdoll against the momentum of the spinning copter. Frost flies out the side.

"Fuck!"

I feel sick. Hicks looks terrified as he struggles to clip his seat belt. I can't reach to help him. Everything leans farther and farther to the left until the left side door is parallel to the ground.

The crash jerks my body violently. Something pops in my shoulder. Dust fills the cabin as the chopper slides across the dirt. Screams mix into the scrap metal as bodies get turned in the debris.

I'm dangling from my seat. The helicopter is on its side, with the right door open to the bright sky. I undo my seat belt and fall onto bloody ground. My shoulder hurts. I failed before I could even start, this is a god damn disaster.

"Remember your mission," I tell myself.

I will not miss my chance to finally be in a real fight. I remember the hours of training during Ranger School, the endless lectures in Special Forces, the constant drills The Colonel put me through. The old man popped my shoulder back in after I dislocated it during a wrestling match with John. I can do it myself this time. I grit my teeth and shove the ball back into the socket with a muffled scream "AH!"

"I'm not done yet."

There's gunfire close by I refuse to miss it because I'm trapped. I need to get out. As I stand I touch a severed limb. The mangled bodies of Hicks, Noob and the two chopper gunners are scattered about. The two gunners were crushed by the weight of the guns impacting them. Noob's head is smashed into his torso, brain matter ooze from his broken helmet. Hicks is breathing but he is unconscious. I can't tell the extent of the damage all his gear on. His legs are caught under the helicopter. I can't move him without any equipment. I only brought was ammo and a camel pack of water. This was supposed to be a simple mission. I maneuver to the cockpit to check the piolet and co-pilot. The co-pilot is dead, nothing left of her face.

The pilot coughs up blood, "Fucking RPG. Hit us right in the tail."

"Jesus Christ, Spunkmeyer! Try not to talk. The steering is in your stomach."

He chuckles, "It's just another happy landing… is..is Ferro alright?"

The co-pilot's name tag says Ferro. I tell him, "Sure…"

He begins to fade. The smell of his bowels voiding fills the cockpit. He's dead. Fuck, I have to find Bishop. He's the only one that can actually help Hicks right now. Once the fight is done we can move the helicopter off of him.

I climb the chairs like a ladder to get out of the cabin. I reach with my left arm but as soon as I put my weight onto it, pain shoots through my body. I have to climb out one handed. I pull myself to the top of the wreckage. As I peek out, I see a massive gunfight. Apone leads men against a well-fortified enemy. I can see that they're trying to get to our crash but there's not enough cover and too much resistance with no air support. The other helicopters fucked right off as soon as ours went down. Apone won't risk an air strike destroying the target.

I can see the enemy's muzzle flashes as they move through their buildings. They don't see me. I take a deep breath as I rest my rifle on the edge of my cover. I will not go quietly. I switch my rifle to semi-auto.

I am wrath. There is no need to spray and pray, for I am ruin. I can make every shot count, for I am doom. I see a muzzle flash. I am death. I instantly fire at the blurry figure behind it. As more figures go to the figure's aid, I put more bullets into that space.

I feel completely hidden, they didn't expect anyone to have survived the crash so they aren't looking my way.

Then the fire from the compound becomes more chaotic. Each time I see a muzzle flash, I end the figure behind it. Until I can't hit any more live targets. They must of changed positions.

I drop my empty magazine and slam in a fresh one. I crawl out of the wreckage, falling onto the dirt in the open.

Apone sees me.

"Covering fire!"

The enemy doesn't care, as bullets hit all around me as I run. Just before I reach Apone. I feel a hard impact on my upper back with a loud ping. I tumble to the ground next to Apone.

He yells, "Man down!"

The impact knocked the wind out of my lungs. For thirty seconds of excruciating pain in my chest I can't breathe. My eye still can't focus no matter how many times I blink.

"Look at me, Kane. Focus on me!"

I try to speak but only grunted sound comes out.

"Hang in there, Kane. You're going to be fine!"

The pain fades as air finally enters my lungs.

"I'm fine." I take a breath. "I'm fine."

Apone smacks my helmet, "That's what body armor is for."

"Where's Bishop? Hicks is still alive in the chopper. I couldn't do anything for him."

Bishop yells from behind nearby cover, "I'm not much help right now. Fell off the rope when the chopper got hit. Broke my dang leg!"

Apone says, "Ain't no one going to be able to get back in there until we finish this fight! Kane, you and five others sweep to the left. Get in the compound. We'll secure the copter until Second Platoon get here. This is on us to win. Now go!"

I sweep around the compound with Hudson and Drake, blasting our way in. This is all routine now. We clear the building, dropping everyone in our way. I step over the bodies from my earlier kill streak. We reach the final room, and Hudson kicks the door down.

Two men scramble through the room. The younger of the two grabs a rifle firing it from the hip. I duck back behind the wall. Hudson isn't quick enough taking one to the thigh. While the fire is focused at me Drake drops him with a burst. I recognize the older one to be the al-Qaeda leader. I fire at his legs as he runs through a doorway. I hear him fall. I run after to find him feebly crawling away with one bullet wound in his calf.

"Asshole!"

I kick him in the face knocking out several teeth. I zip tie his hands behind his back and drag him out.

Drake says, "Hudson's been hit in his femoral artery. If we don't act he'll bleed out in two minutes."

My attention does not leave my prisoner. "You take him. I will not abandon our target."

Drake mutters "Prick" as he lifts Hudson over his shoulders in a fireman carry.

He can insult me all he wants. I will complete this mission no matter what. As I force the injured al-Qaeda leader to hobble out of the room I hear an explosion consistent with a grenade. Great what now?

I sling my rifle and unholster my pistol. I need only one hand on my prisoner to keep him walking. I find the painful truth just down the hall. Drakes shredded body lays on top of Hudson. One of the downed terrorists must have been pretending to be dead, then pulled a grenade when the opportunity arose. Is this my fault was I in too much of a hurry?

No.

"I refuse to take the full blame for this. They were with me. They had just as much of a chance to check for survivors."

Hudson screams, "AAAHHH!" in defiance.

I push the prisoner to the ground face first. Then move Drakes body off of Hudson. "Good god! How are you alive?"

He resists thinking this is a fight for his life.

"It Barry. I'm right here." Trying to calm him.

Hudson is bleeding from all over. The only reason the explosion didn't kill him is because Drake's body shielded him. He reaches to me with a shredded hand, fingers dangle from bits of skin. "Don't let them take me! I'm not ready to go!"

I grab his hand, "I'll get you out of here!"

His grip loosens as he calms down.

"I need to tell Gabby I love her. I need to…"

I let go of the limp hand of another dead friend.

My prisoner laughs out of his broken mouth. I pick him up then punch him in the gut with my pistol. He buckles over, puking up a small amount of liquid. I drag him out of the complex. I find the rest of the platoon finishing the last bits of resistance.

The area is secured as the rest of the Company choppers in. Lieutenant Colonel Cameron lands, receives a quick summary of the fight from Apone and is given custody of the al-Qaeda leader. They leave immediately, staying on the ground for less than a minute.

Captain Weyland stays to clean up the mess with the rest of us. Bishop is flown out with the injured. I refuse to leave until we get Hicks out of that chopper despite my injuries. There is the risk of a retaliation attack if we stay to long. I don't want to miss any of the action. So we set up a parameter as a team of engineers work to remove the bodies out of the wreckage.

As I sit waiting for another fight, the adrenaline that was fueling me wears off. My shoulder aches if I move it even slightly. I keep my arm close to my chest trying to keep all weight off of it. There is sharp pain in my back. I think the metal plate in my armor is dented and rubbing a fresh bruise. I refuse to take out that protection, I accept the pain.

I hear them get out Hicks out as well as the other dead in the copter. I stand up to go to them. With that quick movement my hips burns. I grunt in pain. I look around but I don't think anyone saw my weakness.

Hicks is still breathing. It's faint, and his legs are mangled. The other bodies are covered up. until wind blows the cover off of Noob and Frost. Noob's final moment of pain frozen to his face as it was forced into his torso, forces others to look away. Frost is a crumbled mess, I don't know what he hit when he flew out of the helicopter but the impact broke almost every bone in his body. Hudson's blood soaked body still drips. I wonder who Gabby was, probably his girlfriend back in Montana he was to afraid to tell the truth. Apone stands above them speechless. I don't know what to say to him. He's not crying, so he might be fine. He is a tough guy…right?

CHAPTER 18

DEPLOYMENT END

Back on post I learn Hicks is in a coma and might not wake up. They'll ship him back to the States for better treatment. I can only hope that he makes it but what kind of life awaits him if he wakes up. Forever trapped in a broken body. Unable to clean up after himself. No longer able to interact with the world. A fate worse than death.

I keep running through the mission as I clean my gear. What could I have done differently? I should have put an extra bullet the bodies in the compound. If only that RPG missed. Nothing will bring back my friends. Hudson's blood is still on my hand. I almost don't want to wash it off.

I don't go out on anymore serious missions on this deployment, instead spending all of my time on post waiting for the day to end. Captain Weyland got all the glory for taking a major al-Qaeda leader into custody after the battle, and there's a rumor going around that he's going to get promoted to lieutenant colonel. He has no need to chase glory for the remaining month. Apone acts the same, like nothing has changed despite how quiet everything is now.

My bruises finally fade by the time my deployment ends and we return to the States. My room at Fort Benning feels uncomfortably quiet and empty without the noise of Noob playing video games that I'd grown used to on deployment. I just feel kind of empty. I don't sleep my first night, there's nothing to do until tomorrow night. I just sit on my bed going over everything that happened on deployment from sunset to sunrise. Could I have done more? Running countless scenarios in my head. Until the sun sets once again.

At our post deployment party at the Foxy Lady, we toast our lost friends Noob, Frost, Hudson, and Hicks, who passed away in transport.

Bishop is being medically discharged, having broken his femur, dislocated his hip, and completely disconnected his knee. From a wheelchair, he raises his glass of water. "To my dearest of friends. I will miss you, but I won't miss all of you." He swallows a few pills with his drink.

Everyone laughs and drinks to his toast.

I share a pitcher of Hick's favorite beer with Apone. It tastes less and less disgusting the more you drink, so to solve that problem we drink a lot. You can't buy beer, only rent it.

Lieutenant Gorman grabs me. "Kane, I've got good news for you."

Slurring my words, I reply, "Really? What's happening?"

"You'll be getting a battlefield commission from your actions in taking down that al-Qaeda leader."

"Cool. When's that happening?"

"They'll call you soon, so try not to get too messed up tonight. You don't want to get your first promotion with a hangover." He then looks around to see if we're alone in the restroom. "Also, can you do me a favor?"

"Sure thing, boss." Fuck, it's hard to stay focused.

"Keep an eye on Apone for me. He's starting to worry me. With Hudson and Hicks both gone, plus his wife finally got full custody of the kids, he's been making some bold statements when he thinks he's alone. I don't think he's going to do anything stupid, but just keep an eye on him when I can't."

"You got it, boss. I won't leave his side tonight. We have another pitcher to finish off."

The night is a lot less festive even with the dancers strutting around naked on stage. Apone tells me the story of when he first enlisted.

"It was what I had wanted since I was a kid."

I say, "Same, man. Same."

"As soon as I became a Ranger, I proposed to my high school sweetheart. We had twins, we bought a house…life just started happening. I had no idea she was banging some art major at her college. I came home early after my third deployment and found them in bed. I beat the twerp within an inch of his life. That was so fucking stupid. Then when she filed for divorce, she used that as a reason for why I was unfit to be in my kid's lives. She got everything, fucking everything. Now what? I'm thirty, living on post, giving all my money to a woman who hates me."

I drunkenly say, "That's a lot to take in, dude. I have the opposite problem. I've got no one. Been single for most of my life. I had a girlfriend when my family lived in Florida, but we broke up when I moved to Yuma. The life of a military brat. Never stay anywhere long enough to put down roots."

Apone finishes his beer. "My advice, Kane—don't ever get married. Then when it ends, which it always does, they can't legally take anything." He stands up. "I got to take a piss. Let's get some of these ladies to come home with us."

"Sounds good to me." Then I do a shot of whiskey and the world becomes a blur of laughter and moans of passion. Everything moves around me until darkness takes me.

Then I'm jolted awake. I am immediately ready to fight. "What?!"

Above me stands Apone. "Beer run. How good are you to drive?"

My head hurts, but the room isn't spinning. I could throw up, but I don't feel it at the back of my throat. I look at my hands, finding everything is in focus. I slap myself awake. "Why didn't you grab anyone else for this?"

Apone says, "Because everyone else, including me, is still too drunk. And you're new enough to still be looking to impress. Also, she needs to leave before someone less cool than me finds her." He tosses his keys to me.

A beautiful woman is smiling next to me. Must have been a great night, but too bad I can't remember much.

She says, "You were fun last night." She winks at me as we get dressed. "I'm Destiny, by the way."

I nod stupidly, unable to believe I got too drunk to remember the night I had with this beautiful woman.

"Don't worry, it's not my first time having to sneak out of this place."

I hope I didn't catch anything. I'll have to go by medical later.

Saturday afternoon traffic is rough, plus I feel like absolute shit. Apone also demands that we go to the grocery store on the other side of town. His reason is that it will have what he's looking for. My head hurts too much to argue.

Apone says, "Check out separately so they don't check your ID. There's something I have to take care of first."

"Yeah, sure. My goal is something full of caffeine and electrolytes." Then I turn down the beverage aisle, almost bumping into someone's cart.

I stare at the dozens of different drinks on display for too long, not sure what flavor I want, and end up getting a blue Powerade and a Red Bull. As I walk to the check out, I have to lean on a shelf and feel like I could puke. Then I hear yelling. *Oh great. What now?*

"Do you know what you took from me, bitch?!"

I know that voice. *Oh shit! Who is Apone yelling at?* I start running to the front, expecting to have to back him up in a fight.

Someone yells, "Gun!" followed up by high-pitched screams.

People run past me in terror. *Oh shit! Oh fuck!* Then I see Apone pointing a pistol at a woman behind the register. I yell, "Wait, Apone!"

His eyes locked on her, he says, "This is what you took from me." He points the gun at his own head and fires. His blood peppers the ground as he falls dead.

After the cops interrogate me, I go back to post where the news has already reach command. I am left in a waiting room alone as my commanding officers decided what to do next. I place my head in my hands.

This is not how it was supposed to go. I'm a Kane, god

damn it. I'm a born killer. It is my family's legacy. I am meant to be able to cut these attachments. I'm meant to climb to glory with this ability just like my father before me. Instead, I've just watched my friend kill himself in front of his ex-wife.

Fuck, why is everything so fucked up?

Lieutenant Gorman comes out and sits across from me. "No one ever told you where Apone's ex-wife worked. I feared something like this coming after Hicks and Hudson died."

I don't say anything. I failed my mission.

When I go into Lieutenant Colonel Cameron's office, I stand at attention, composing myself as best I can.

He says, "Specialist Barry Kane, you have proven to be a fine soldier. I knew of your father and his achievements. Is it true he got those scars from a tiger?"

"Yes, sir. He has told me the story many times."

"You proved instrumental in the capture of a high-ranking al-Qaeda leader in Iraq. Unfortunately, with you having been present at Staff Sergeant Apone's suicide, you will be transferred from my regiment. To put simply, it would be disheartening to the other men."

You mean it makes you look bad. You pompous ass. One of your men offed himself when you knew this was a possibility. You handed the responsibility to someone below you rather than sending him for a psychological evaluation because that could look poorly for you. Now you can't afford to simply discharge me, not with my Special Forces training, because the army hasn't gotten its full investment yet. I want to say that so badly, but it wouldn't be worth it. At least I'm not being court-martialed.

He stands up and hands me a folder of papers. "Good-bye, Corporal Kane."

"Wait, why am I being promoted?"

He says, "Your new regiment needed a Corporal, so we promoted you to fill that void." He salutes me.

I salute back. Maybe this isn't so bad.

CHAPTER 19

ANGEL'S MACHINE

HAVE BEEN AWAKE FOR SEVENTY-TWO hours, surviving purely on caffeine and junk food full of sugar. My court summons is coming up soon, and I can't waste any time, even though time will have a new meaning when I am done.

The charges have been pressed, but I remain free one week before my pretrial, when the judge will decide whether I wait behind bars for the trial or continue to be free. I'm too close to a breakthrough to waste any of my time. Francisco couldn't convince our former employer to drop the arson charges against me. By charging me with arson for the destruction of his restaurant, he will receive more money from the insurance, even though he authorized me to fix the oven. The destruction of little Angel's life means nothing to him if he can make more money. It was a simple mistake, but I don't care anymore. My goal is far beyond something so trivial. I'm about to change the world, maybe even more than that.

I have almost finished the machine. The simulations

show that it should work. I was forgetting to include space with calculations of time, which also requires way more power. I removed all possible inhibitors from the tests. Jason didn't just travel to a parallel universe existing in the past. His mind had to move a massive distance to the parallel universe. Since it would still take billions of years to even travel between galaxies at the speed of light. His mind must have skipped the distance. I am about to open that truth.

My hands are covered in blisters, burns, and small cuts. When the caffeine and sugar wear off, I'll be sick for a week.

None of my discomfort matters now though, only progress.

I'm creating a tear within our own world with pure energy focused in upon itself. That's what Jason did. His thoughts were ripped from his original life and transferred to our world all from the energy of a nuclear explosion. Now I shall recreate it, but rather than transferring my thoughts to a parallel version of myself, I shall create a window to the parallel world.

The hardest part was the computer wiring to ensure the correct frequencies are generated. I gained full access to the city's power grid far too easily. The password was simply Password123. Only an idiot couldn't figure that out.

With the final bolt tightened, I gaze upon my masterpiece. It stands seven feet tall and seven feet wide and is made of mix-matched parts. I go to the computer to prepare the uplink and then finally remove the cover I put over the security cameras. I want a record of only the results, nothing about building it so I remain needed for the creation. I suspect Mr. Lock and Professor Knight are conspiring against me. I will never give them the opportunity to succeed without me.

My stomach feels weird, the combination of nerves starting to get to me and the toxic concoction of junk fueling me. I take a deep breath.

"This will work. I know it will." I give a thumbs up to the security camera. "Here we go."

I press Enter and turn the machines power switch on. The machine buzzes to life. I wish I had hearing protection as it grows louder with more power. Sparks flash as energy shoots from the cross-connecting wires and a sphere of energy forms in the center.

"It's working!" At least I think it is. I'm honestly not sure what the final result will look like. What if I open a portal to the nuclear holocaust that is the remains of Jason's old world?

Then the room's lights glow extremely bright just before shattering and the machine starts to break in half.

"Shit!" I shouldn't have used duct tape.

I run to my machine in a feeble attempt to hold it together. "Come on! I need you to work!"

With my head only a foot from the center as I hold the side wanting to fall away, I see a reflection of myself on a glass-like floating ball. Is this it? I want to reach out and touch it, but my arms are the only thing holding everything together. Yet my eyes are fixed on this clear ball.

My grip loosens as my arms are pulled farther apart. The reflective surface also pulls apart, resulting in two floating spheres. I let go with my right arm as the piece begins to get too far away, switching to my right leg to hold it together. With my free arm, I reach out to one of the floating mirrors.

My hand slides through it with no resistance whatsoever, as if I'm reaching into a puddle of water. Then my hand comes out the other sphere pointing directly back at me. I move my arm up and shove it deeper into the sphere, then watch my arm come out the other sphere pointing down. My fingers move as if they were not separated by a space between the two spheres of pure energy. With one more push, I can scratch my own nose.

My grip of the machine loosens further. I pull my arm from the spheres, confirming that my hand is unchanged.

Then the machine splits in two, pulling the spheres into two floating orbs. With power still holding them in place, I take the pencil from my pocket and throw it into one of the spheres, now three feet from the other. The pencil pops out the opposite sphere without losing any speed. I then stand in between the two floating spheres and throw my shoe at one, just to have it fly out the other one and hit me in the back. I examine the shoe. It is without a doubt mine. It smells just like me.

"Holy shit! I did it! I really did it!"

Then the cables short out. The machine's power fades and the spheres disappear.

I turn to the security camera and bow. "Behold, for I have changed the world."

CHAPTER 20

BACK TO JUVIE

LEFT AN ECSTATIC MESSAGE ON Professor Knight's desk.

I did it! The portal worked. I created teleportation! Look at the security footage. It's all there. But only I have the knowledge to recreate it. I can't do it again if I'm incarcerated. Better get me a good lawyer.

~ The genius creator Angel Molina

Then I cleared the computer and removed the hard drive. The security camera is now the only recording of the test. I alone hold the knowledge of how to create what I am calling "Angel's Window." Jason's Window doesn't have the same inspiration behind it.

Now the university can't afford to risk me going back to prison. Administrators will spend as much money as possible on lawyers to keep me from being incarcerated. I'll never see the inside of a cell again. I'm simply worth too much.

As my pretrial hearing approaches, I'm not worried. Francisco has pleaded with his old boss, calling the man every day, but it's no use. One day at home after a heated argument, Francisco ends the call by yelling, "Fuck you! You greedy asshole!" and throwing his phone across the room where it embeds itself into the thin wall.

From the hallway I say, "You worry too much. Trust me, everything will work out."

It takes him a few moments to regain his composure. "I am the correct amount of worried. How can you be this calm? Do you have any idea what an arson charge like this will do to you? You could spend the next decade of your life in prison."

"The world can't afford to let me get locked up. I've changed everything in the past week. And the only place the numbers exist are here in my head, in my notebook, and these hard drives." *Which have not left my sight.*

"Angel, we haven't had any contact with the university since the charges were filed. How do you know they haven't just abandoned you?"

I simply say, "Trust me. At the hearing, everything will work out." For I have a friend who has seen the future, which now is guaranteed to include me.

Before the hearing, my mother and I meet with my public defender to look over the case. She's in her early thirties, with long blonde hair and her eyes are bloodshot from lack of sleep.

"I'm Carrie Watters. Sorry we didn't have time to speak sooner. I'm currently working five cases. What are we pleading?"

I say, "Not guilty." I bet my real lawyer will be here after the hearing.

Carrie skims through my paperwork while drinking

dark black coffee. "Angel, I don't think that will work. Judge Dredd is known for giving maximum sentences. With your two prior convictions, you will be tried as an adult. If you plead guilty, you will get a much lighter sentence and could be out by the time you're eighteen."

Insulted, I say, "Hell no! I didn't do anything wrong. I was given permission to fix the oven by the manager himself. It was all under his supervision. The entire kitchen staff witnessed it. I may have fucked up, but he watched me use tape to fix the wires. This is just as much his fault as it is mine. I am not getting thrown back in the joint because of this bullshit. And where the hell is the university's lawyer? They can't afford to have me sent away."

My mom puts her hand on my shoulder. "Calm down, Angel. She's trying her best to help."

"No, this is all bullshit! I've discovered wormhole travel. I should be on the front page of the newspaper, selling my discovery to the government for billions!"

Mom says, "Getting angry won't change this." She turns to my defender. "My boyfriend was working the night of the fire. He can testify that Angel was being watched by the manager, Raúl."

Carrie Watters asks, "Was he in the kitchen and saw all this happen?"

Mom says, "I don't know. He was a waiter, so he could've been out taking customer's orders."

"If that's the case, his testimony will likely be thrown out as hearsay. We need people who were there with concrete proof. It also doesn't help that Angel was not a registered employee. In the eyes of the law, he wasn't supposed to be in the kitchen at all. And the prosecution will twist that to make you seem like a sinister character."

I say, "Baldeo was there!"

Mom leans in to whisper to me, "Baldeo is an illegal immigrant. He'll be deported back to Mexico if he comes to court."

"Please don't whisper. I need to hear everything that can help the case. Nothing will leave this room. It all falls under client confidentiality, I promise."

Mom returns to normal volume and says, "Baldeo's situation prevents him from testifying. My boyfriend and I have been trying to gather support from the rest of the staff to help Angel, but unfortunately, Raúl is promising them all work once he rebuilds and none of them want to jeopardize their jobs."

"So I'm on my own. My word against his. I'm just a repeat Hispanic delinquent in their eyes..." With a sarcastic chuckle, I acknowledge, "I'm screwed."

Carrie says, "Plead guilty. We'll be able to have at least two of the felony charges dropped and you'll be free just as soon as you become an adult. You will still be tried as an adult and you'll spend your time in prison rather than juvenile detention, but you will be kept separate from the adults until midnight of your eighteenth birthday."

I stare down at the floor. "I don't think I've ever been free." I didn't want to risk my notebook, so I wrap it in a plastic bag with the hard drives before burying it next to the trailer.

Francisco watches me dig the hole as he works on his car.

I say, "If I don't get out, I don't want anyone using it other than me." Then I cover the hole with dirt.

The hearing is full of other people giving their pleas. Judge Dredd shows no remorse as he gives out sentences to everyone who pleads guilty. Then it is my turn to stand at the podium, looking up to the judge in his black robe. Carrie stands at the podium with me. Mom waits in the back of the room for moral support. Francisco stayed at home to watch my younger siblings and because he would probably do something, as he said, "Stupid and dangerous."

Judge Dredd says, "Angel Luna Molina, you are accused of arson for burning down a family-owned restaurant. This was an occupied structure worth over two hundred thousand dollars, a value set by the insurance company. You face three felony charges, including arson, destruction of property and endangering the lives of the occupants, with a maximum sentence of twelve years. Do you understand the charges against you?"

I say, "I do."

"As a sixteen year old, you requested to be tried as a juvenile. You are a repeat offender with two prior convictions on your record. I have no tolerance of someone who has squandered their second chance, let alone a third chance. You have felt the repercussions of your illegal actions too many times to be considered a juvenile. As such, I hereby reject your request and you will be charged as an adult. How do you plead?"

Carrie says, "We plead guilty with the condition that two of the charges are dropped."

He doesn't take long to consider the offer. "Very well. Angel Molina will be held at the Maricopa County jail for the next three years to repay his debt to society." Then he bangs his gavel. "I'm sure I'll be seeing you again. Next case."

I am handcuffed and led out of the courtroom. As they take me away, I look back to see Mom quietly crying as she tries her best to not make a scene. This is the first time she's seen me arrested.

I've been through this enough to know the whole routine. They take everything from me and do a complete search of my body, but this time I'm given an orange jumpsuit instead of keeping my civilian clothes. I stand in a line with grown men to board a bus and be driven to the downtown jail. The university abandoned me.

"God, please get me out of this," I pray for the first time in years.

I have to stay at the courthouse jail here in Phoenix, but at least I'm kept separate from the adults. Not by much though. They yell profanities through the bars, like, "I'll see you in Tent City, little boy!" and they make moaning sounds.

My cell reminds me of the one in Yuma. Long brick hallways painted white. It all feels too familiar. I need to get out. As soon as I sit down in my cell, I am told I have a visitor.

I assume it's Mom or Francisco, but instead, Professor Knight waits on the other side of a plastic window, smiling, so I bet he has good news.

I ask, "Did you get me letter?"

"I did. Truly unbelievable what was accomplished. A new hope for humanity. Now not even the stars are our limits."

"Thank you. So when is the university sending their legal team to get me out?"

"They're not," he says in a deadpan tone.

We sit in silence for a long moment, then I lean in closer to the hole in the plastic window in case I didn't hear him right. "What?"

"I'm sorry to say, the university will not be helping you. Hell, I'm only here now to say goodbye. And Lock wanted me to give you this letter, but I can't exactly hand it to you."

He takes out a letter from his clean brown jacket, then clears his throat. "Glad you're where you belong, you filthy criminal." He looks it over. "That's it? Well, I guess that's why he teaches math and not English."

I punch the glass. "You can't cut me out! I'm the only one who knows the equations."

The corrections officers move in, ready to take me down.

Professor Knight waves them away. "It's alright, gentlemen. He's only hurting himself."

My hand trembles with pain.

"We don't need you to actually open the portals. The fact that we have proof that it is possible is all we need. The US Government has given us a five billion dollar grant and a ten year contract to recreate the results. That's a full career, and I have enough of a basic idea of the equations that I bet I can make it work. Even if we can't recreate the portals, I'll be able to live in wealth for the rest of my life. You are no longer needed."

"*Que te den cabrón!*" I throw myself at the window with all of my weight, just to bounce off and only hurt myself. "You better pray I never get out!"

The corrections officers swarm me. A baton hits the back

of my thighs, dropping me to my knees, and then they drag me a way.

"That's *my* work, *not* yours!"

They throw me into my cell after a couple of extra hits.

I will not let them get away with this. When I get out, I'll destroy every aspect of what they stole from me.

Then again, the government has the outlines of the technology. Does that mean Jason's future war is stopped, or does that just mean the war will be fought with teleporting weapons? I shouldn't care, but I will not be cheated out of what is rightfully mine.

CHAPTER 21

SHIVERING IN THE COLD AND in chains, I stand outside of a chain link fence covered in barbed wire with five other men. Attached over the gate into the prison is big pink sign that reads Joe Arpaio Tent City. The corrections officer commands us to state our names as we pass.

Moving now, I say, "Angel Luna Molina."

Then I am processed into the facility and given a black and white shirt and pants. Pink underwear, pink socks, pink towels, pink pillow, and two pink blankets because it's getting cold.

I ask, "Why pink?"

The corrections officer chuckles. "What's wrong, too girly for you? All inmates wear pink."

I understand it's to emasculate us, but if everyone is wearing pink, then it will be something to bond over. If you wanted to embarrass a man with pink, make only him wear it.

I take in everything at this guard station. It's not exactly a building, more like an open metal shed with fans and an impressive air conditioning unit and large portable heaters. I'm guessing only they get to be comfortable in this desert climate. Every guard has a taser gun and a wooden baton. I see a high-powered gas gun behind the desk with boxes of ammo labeled pepper balls.

I am taken to a green twenty-man tent separated by its own covered fence topped with thick razor wire. The juvenile tent has eleven occupants of different races. Here we can interact, but I know once we are brought into the main population, we will stick to our races. That's how it was in Juvie. Thankfully, I had my cousin David to protect me. Then Jason, after David got shanked. I wish I had that crazy white boy here now. I'll just have to fend for myself for the next three years.

My seventeenth birthday is a few weeks away. With the timing of my sentence, I'll still have two years to serve after I turn eighteen. I can handle delinquents my age, but a career criminal with a gang of fighters behind them and nothing to lose scares me. I'll have to tough it out if I want my rightful place in history.

I join a game of Spades, but no one is betting anything. Ending up in someone's debt is dangerous. Even more so if they are in a rival gang. Two of the inmates playing cards are from Mexico. Santos has a tear tattoo under his eye. He's a drug mule who got busted crossing the border. He's twitchy, makes me uncomfortable. The other Mexican, Salvador, is much more calm. He was looking for work when he got picked up crossing the border.

"I've got a baby mama back home and no job," he tells me in Spanish. At least that's what I think he says. I'm out of practice. He continues, "I turn eighteen tonight. I don't know how long I'll be here before I get shipped back."

The third guy playing is a white boy the others call Roach. He asks, "What's he saying, new meat?"

Apparently I'm the only one who can translate here. "He's going over to the adult population tonight."

Roach says, "Rough. I still have another twenty days till then. I'm going to have trouble keeping my salt supply hidden."

"Is salt contraband?"

They all nod.

Roach says, "Salt, pepper, even sugar are all banned. Fucking Shitler in charge feeds us pig slop, then bans anything to help the flavor. He boasts about how more money is spent on dog food than the inmates."

Night air flows by me, chilling me to my core.

The correction's officer yells, "Lights out!"

I wrap myself with every piece of fabric I have but am still cold. Sleep does not come to me as I shiver under the neon Vacancy sign on the guard tower. The point of using tents instead of building a prison is to cut costs. Expanding a prison for an influx of prisoners costs tens of thousands of dollars. Setting up more military surplus tents is cheap. There's a faded stamp from 1950 on the flap. The Vacancy sign is Sheriff Joe Arpaio's cruelest joke. He once said, "I will put up more tents before I let anyone get out early."

Morning comes and we are sent to clean up before breakfast. Some inmates shower quick so they can grab a few minutes of shut eye inside the mess hall. Food is a tray of green slop. Mushy food with a green tint. The only meat is a green slice of stiff ham. It tastes as good as it looks. I swear the cheese slice is plastic. It makes me miss cabbage soup. Now I see why Roach smuggled in salt.

The inmate next to me yells, "I'd rather starve than eat this shit!" He throws his tray at a guard.

Everyone moves out of the way.

Pepper balls are fired, smacking the inmate in the chest. He charges the gunmen before being tased and taken down. A stay ball hits me in the shoulder. The impact feels like I got punched by a grown man, and the pepper makes my eyes burn like I've been pepper sprayed.

As the inmate is dragged off, he yells, "Take me to solitaire! I get to sleep inside!"

I'm given a new shirt and my eyes are washed before I get my work assignment. My shoulder has a bruise the size of my fist. My eyes still burn a bit, but I guess this is how my day is going to be. Work is going to suck.

We are chained together and then marched onto a bus.

Our guard states, "Today is a special day. We have a new worker, Angel." He points to me. "Welcome to the only prison in Arizona that still does a chain gang. Everyone works in this prison. No one gets a free ride. Today you'll be digging graves. The lost souls of this city do not have a family to bury them. Today you are their family. Treat them with respect."

We spend nine hours digging six-foot deep holes in a dirt lot. I hate how in Arizona it can be blazing hot during the day and freezing cold at night. By the end, everyone has a layer of dirt coated on them. I have fresh blisters on my hands from trying to break through the caliche dirt, which is as hard as concrete. Everyone has to work together to carry the caskets to their holes. Roach says a prayer as the hole is filled.

Death feels too close. I don't want to die here. I want to get back what is rightfully mine so I can give my family a better life. I don't want my half-brother and sister to grow up like I had to. I want my mom to not have to work. I want to buy Francisco a car he doesn't have to work on constantly.

As we are brought back to Tent City, we are all exhausted. How the heck am I going to survive two years of this? There are some adults getting searched against the fence. Now I know the procedure when our tent gets raided. I stop the chain gang's synchronized march as I see the one person I never wanted to see again. I rub my eyes, hoping that it's just the pepper spray from earlier, but I see perfectly fine.

My father's eyes lock onto mine. He's lost weight, looking more dangerous than before. He takes one hand off the fence to slide his thumb across his neck as he silently mouths the words, "You're dead."

I can't breathe. He's going to kill me. I don't stand a chance in here even if I join a rival gang. Once the word gets out that I testified against him, I'm fucking dead.

I'm hit in the back. "Keep moving!"

My eye's stay fixed on Renato until we turn the corner back into our section of Tent City.

I don't sleep at all despite how tired I am. Could he have paid off someone in my tent to strike? I can't leave myself vulnerable for a single second. How the hell am I going to survive two years here?

The sun doesn't rise. Instead, cold rain falls from the sky. We are sent to clean up before chow. I don't look at my slop as I eat. My eyes dart around the room for a possible attack. Everyone is attached to the chain gang except for me.

"Do I get a day off or something?"

The corrections officer says, "You have a visitor."

"Cool."

Is the guard being paid by Renato? I can't say no. They'll just take me by force. If I have to fight, I can't waste energy here.

I'm taken into the building at the center of Tent City, passing by the main surveillance room and the guard sleeping at his desk. Should I try to escape? I am left alone in a small conference room. Is this where Renato is going to have me killed? I need a weapon. I don't have much time, as I search every corner of the room for anything useful. All I find is a plastic pen under the table. I stand up with my back against the far wall as a bald man in a black suit and sunglasses comes in with a black briefcase.

Who wears sunglasses inside? This guy must take himself way too seriously. He looks like an assassin from a movie.

He looks me up and down.

Feeling awkward, I say, "So…what's the plan?" I hold the pen behind me tightly. I'll stab him in the eye as soon as he gets close.

The man sits at the table. "Well, I had a plan. But because of you that has changed."

I can't place his accent, maybe European. There's definitely frustration behind it.

"What did I do to upset you?"

He opens his briefcase and pulls out my notebook. "Did you make this?"

I instinctively reach for it and thumb through the pages. "This is mine. How did you find it?"

"I asked your family nicely. They were more than willing to tell me when I said it would help you get out of here."

I hold my notebook close. "Did you convince the kitchen staff to tell the truth to prove my innocence?"

"I'm not your lawyer."

"Then who are you?"

He smiles, revealing perfect teeth. "I'm here to offer you a job. If you accept it, the charges will be dropped and we'll walk out of here right now. You'll never see the inside of another prison cell ever again."

"That sounds great…wait. You don't work for the university, do you? Are you a government agent?"

"You could say that."

"So if I were to say no, would I *disappear*?" I emphasize disappear to sound scary.

He says, "I'll put this simply. Do you want out or not? Because no one is coming to save you. Your university colleagues were trying to copyright these formulas in their names. I figured out who you were through blurry security camera footage."

Government work was probably going to be the result anyway, and if I stay here, Renato will get me. I reply, "Alright, deal. But as long as I get full credit for it and it's called Angel's Window."

"That's fine."

He knocks on the door. It opens, revealing two other men in black suits and ties who then escort me out of the room and down a completely empty hallway. I look into the security room and see the same guard still asleep. There's also a third agent doing something to the computer. It looks like he's clearing the footage. They take me out the front gate and into a black SUV with black-tinted windows.

Who are these people? I clutch my notebook even tighter. *Where are the hard drives?*

The bald man climbs in the back seat with me. "Relax, we need you more than the notebook."

I ask, "So which branch do you guys work for? CIA, FBI, or Secret Service?"

"You're thinking small. Those organizations work for us. What you've built has changed everything. Our big secrets will have to be revealed, unfortunately. I never thought it would come this soon."

I want to ask more, but I'm more concerned with where they're taking me. I watch out the window for a while, soon realizing they are taking me to the airport.

"Shouldn't I be going to see my family?"

The bald man says, "No, there are more pressing matters."

"No there aren't. I won't just abandon my family."

The bald man takes off his sunglasses, revealing red eyes with oval pupils. They look more like goat eyes than human. "Yes, there are."

"What's wrong with your eyes?"

"It's a very painful story."

"Are you an alien? Am I being abducted?"

He puts his sunglasses back on. "No, I am very much human. In fact, your invention will be what saves all of humanity."

CHAPTER 22

THE TRUTH

THEY TAKE ME TO A private plane on the tarmac. It's not very big, but it's a jet. I'm still in my black and white inmate clothing. I had hoped when I finally got to travel in style, I would look more dignified. But I will take what I can get right now. The cabin has a couch and a set of seats in the front half. A bar that has expensive-looking drinks fills the back just in front of the lavatory. The other agents don't board, leaving me and the bald man with red eyes alone on the plane.

He speaks to the pilot before closing the door. I've never been on a plane before. As the plane begins to roll, I take one of the seats that has a seat belt and click myself in. The bald man just walks to the back and makes himself a drink. Speed increases as we lift off, and I feel my stomach in my throat by the time we soar into the sky. We level off above the clouds. My knuckles had turned white from how hard I was squeezing the armrest.

The bald man walks back to the front of the plane, sipping on a clear drink that smells like bleach. He puts his sunglasses in his shirt pocket. "Welcome to first class. A lot of people have tried to see the inside of this plane. It's not a big deal. I try to keep it minimalist. No need for portable supercomputers anymore. I just need a cell phone to know what's going on."

"Where are we going?"

"The Nevada desert."

"You're taking me to Area 51, aren't you? With all the top secret alien spacecraft?"

"Sure, but that's not its actual name. That's just what the public calls it. That failed weather balloon in 1947 made everyone look to the sky expecting aliens. They have no idea of the horrors really out there." He sits down on the couch, takes another sip.

There's something wrong about his hands, but I can't quiet place it. He has five fingers including a thumb. He doesn't have any fingernails. White hairless skin covers his hands.

"You get to know the truth because you are now top secret. Only I and five other people know about you. You developed something that doesn't exist anywhere else in the galaxy. That tips the balance of power. Soon we will become a target." He cradles his drink in both hands. "You have both saved humanity from being trapped on Earth and doomed us to a war we are not prepared for."

I ask, "A war with who? You make it sound like aliens are going to attack."

That's not the future Jason told me about. Humans were going to fight each other. The portal was meant to stop it all.

"They are. I wish for the days of ignorance, but those are long gone. We have made too many strides forward, learning too much too quickly. We are a small species on a small planet far from anything, doomed to an existence on a planet that had already been killed billions of years ago. They knew we could never truly reach outside our solar system. We were nothing but entertainment."

He finishes his drink. "But that's what's makes us interesting. We have survived disasters and apocalypses. We developed technology that they never even dreamed of. We are far smarter than they can accept and far more resilient. Now, with your new tech, we will take our rightful place in the universe." He then asks, "How did you come up with it?"

I'm sticking to my lie. "It came to me in a dream. I saw a parallel world and knew I could reach it. So are we going to use Angel's Window to colonize other planets?"

"Far more than that."

I look out the windows as we descend toward a long runway with large hangers in a valley surrounded by small mountains. There aren't any roads in or out.

After landing, the man with red eyes escorts me into a hanger on the far end of the grounds. A dozen people gathering equipment all stop and salute the bald man.

"You still haven't told me your name," I say.

"The closest pronunciation to my name is Yabechun. Welcome to your new home. From here, we will provide you with everything you need to recreate your window. You were able to do it yourself in few days before. I will provide you with a team of scientists, engineers, and unlimited resources. I want you to make it sustainable and able to travel."

"That's going to be hard. The original build actually took almost two years before it was operational. The security camera footage was the result of a week without sleep and burning out the Phoenix power grid."

Yabechun says, "Don't worry about power. We can generate more than that here." He begins to leave. "You have three days before other plans will pass the point of no return. Don't disappoint me."

"Wait, wait wait. I need more than three days. Those last three days were fueled by caffeine and sugar. If you want a sustainable movable machine, I need more time than that."

He says loud enough so everyone in the hanger hears us, "You have seventy-three hours." He then leans down to me. "Don't waste my time like your teachers did."

CHAPTER 23

NEW UNIT

"WELL, BARTHOLOMEW KANE, THIS IS the end of your military carrier," I say to myself as I'm being transferred halfway across the country. At least I'm used to starting over. My family really prepared me for that. The Colonel transferred from Marine base to Marine base four times after I was born. I've gotta stop thinking of Dad as The Colonel, since he got promoted to General. It's just a hard habit to break. I tell myself I'll be fine. All my friends are gone. My two deployments were underwhelming. The global war on terror is dying down. Uncle Rob was right—there is no glory for the second son.

I'm on a cargo plane with a bunch of wooden boxes covered with green tarps. I sit against the wall with my bag of stuff. I don't own much. I'll be issued new gear at my new post. I've held on to the important stuff that I can never have too much of, like socks and underwear. As the only passenger, I can lie across the bench. It beats flying commercial. It's free, plus I have leg room.

My destination is Fort Hood. I've heard rumors of that

place. None painted it in a good light. It has the highest crime and murder rate for on-post personal. Plus, it was the setting for a comic strip about a dead military career that I used to read in the morning paper as a kid, called *Beetle Bailey.*

After a long flight, we have a longer layover somewhere in the middle of the country to change out the cargo. No one tells me where, but my guess based on the flight time and the trees would be somewhere in Colorado. Eventually, we touch down on an airfield in the center of a valley. This doesn't look like Texas. Fort Hood should only have mountains.

Crap, I think I took the wrong flight.

I try to explain the situation to someone who looks to be in charge, but he directs me to someone else, who directs me to someone else. Finally, a civilian contractor points me in the direction of Captain Kane's office.

"That sneaky son of a bitch."

I don't knock when I get to his office. I burst in, shouting, "John!"

But his office is empty.

I check behind the door. Where the hell is he? I sit at his desk, liking his really comfortable office chair. I put my feet on his desk and take in the view. It's not a big office and has only a simple desk, computer, and no windows. His file cabinet has sturdy padlock on it.

While admiring a picture of John and Victoria partying in what looks like Las Vegas, I hear him say, "I hope you're comfortable."

I leave my feet on his desk as I look over at him standing in the doorway. "Very comfortable. Thank you very much."

He smacks my feet off his desk. "Move it, shorty. You're getting dirt everywhere."

We switch spots. He brushes his desk clean.

I say, "It's good to see you. Sorry I haven't reached out in a while."

John says, "Don't worry about it. The job takes us away for long stretches of time. You haven't missed much. Austin's in high school, dealing with that drama. Mom and The Colonel are bickering more than normal with his promotion and potential move to DC."

I say, "Remember, he's not a colonel anymore."

"I know, but let's be honest, Dad was never going to willingly retire."

All things I already know.

"And Victoria is pregnant."

"How can you say that so calmly? Congratulations, big bro. Are you ready to be a dad? Is it a boy or a girl?" I walk around his desk and pat him on the back. "When did you and Victoria get hitched?"

He smiles. "It all just happened. She was happy to move to Nevada with me. We got married in Vegas two weeks ago. Then she took the test a few days ago. You're the first person I've told."

"Well, it is an honor to know. I won't tell anyone." I wink at him.

John asks me to close the door. "I'm sure you're wondering why you're here."

"Yeah, I thought I was supposed be checking in with a unit at Fort Hood. And you said Nevada. Am I on a secret base? And how does a Navy SEAL change my assignment?"

"I've been tasked with building a Special Forces Unit

with a wide variety of skills. You fall under that umbrella with your Special Forces tab. Plus, with your forced transfer, I decided to recruit you. Trust me, where they were sending you to, you wouldn't see any more action unless there was a world war. I chose you not just because you're my brother, but also because I need someone with raid experience in a combat zone. And, I know I can trust you."

"So this isn't just nepotism? Is that also how I got that Special Forces mission in Iraq?"

"That was Dad pulling strings to get you additional experience." He unlocks his file cabinet and hands me a contract.

I look through the stipulations, seeing it will bind me to a top secret unit in simple terms. "What are we going to be doing?" I look him dead in the eyes. "Who do we answer to?"

My brother says, "Both of those are top secret. Do you trust me?"

"I want to, I really do." How do I say this honestly? "But I don't know. You have ditched me before."

"Are you still holding a grudge from that party four years ago? In my defense, it was the first night I got to spend with my smoking hot girlfriend after being deployed for months. I'm sorry I wasn't paying attention to my phone. If it means that much to you, I can pay you back the thirty bucks."

His face hardens. "I know all about what happened to your last unit. War is fucked, always has been. Dad got attacked by a damn tiger on a night patrol and had to kill the beast with a knife. Uncle Rob got hit by napalm from a US airstrike. I watched a car full of my friends explode over an IED. My last mission, Operation Neptune Spear, I had to shoot through another person to kill my target. I got on that mission thanks to Dad's influence. Now I have the highest-value kill in the United States military.

"This is who we are. We are Kanes. We are fighters. We are killers. We get the mission done no matter what. I'm giving you a grand opportunity. You can spend the next eight years of your life doing nothing, waiting for your enlistment to end, or you can sign the damn contract."

I sit quietly for a while. I want to say something clever, but nothing comes to mind. Being overseas in a combat zone was the only place that felt remotely like a real home, even though everything went so terribly wrong. I can't spend the next decade just waiting for my enlistment to end. I take the pen from his desk.

"You know, your bedside manners suck." I sign the contract.

CHAPTER 24

ANGEL'S WINDOW MARK II

"**F**OR THE LAST TIME, THE window is generated purely through frequency and power. There are no particles. Stop trying to add your shit to my work!"

The scientist going by the name of Doctor Blue says, "Well, I don't understand how else to make it work. Clearly you don't understand how physics work, Mr. Molina."

"For the love of God, stop calling me Mr. Molina. I hate the man who gave me that name. It's Angel. Just Angel. Or you can just leave. That would make all of our lives so much easier."

I gesture to all the other scientists and engineers quietly working on their tasks to get my machine built. "Yabechun put me in charge of this because I actually made the window. And I did so alone, with junk and duct tape. Your only job is to make sure the power is exactly as I specified."

Blue says, "But everything breaks down to particles."

My patience has run out. I shout, "Frequency is power,

which makes everything! It binds us to every moment that holds us! Now get out of here!"

I am too close to the end to waste anymore time on doubters who are unable to take the risks to make real progress on their own.

The military guards drag him away. No less than ten minutes later, a new person replaces him. He says to call him Doctor Purple and gives me all the information I need on the power generator. I like this feeling.

The final design looks much more professional than what I built in Phoenix. Metal is welded together instead of duct taped and glued, and it's painted white with smooth surfaces. The power sources are two nuclear reactors, each roughly the size of a school bus. They seem oddly small. When I think of nuclear power, I picture full-scale power plants that power an entire state. I'd bet this technology isn't for anyone outside this base though.

On the third day, the machine is powered by both reactors warming up at exactly the same time. Output matches perfectly with my formulas. The window forms exactly as before, but this time, it has a six-foot diameter, matching this larger machine's frame. When we pull the two ends of the machine apart, the reflective sphere divides in two. The spheres maintain the same size no matter how far we separate them. We stop at twenty feet. With normal lighting, I can see my creation perfectly. Each is a mirror of the other.

Everyone stands in awe.

I take a pencil from Doctor Purple's limp hand. He was trying to take notes but became distracted by the sight of the impossible. He doesn't react until I throw it at the window. The pencil flies out the other window instantaneously.

I turn to everyone who has spent the last seventy hours recreating my work. "I give you Angel's Window to the Future. Now, nowhere is beyond our reach." I step forward to walk through my window.

People shout to get me to stop. Someone says, "We're not ready for human testing yet!"

I don't care. This is my destiny. I have to be the first one to go through. After so much failure, after so much mediocrity, nothing will stop me now. I know this will work. I've reached through before.

Keeping my eyes open, I see an endless line of other versions of myself ahead of me, all existing in the same moment. None of us looks back as we pass through to the other end of the portal.

I stand facing everyone with their dumb-struck faces. I bow, and they all clap.

I have changed the world.

CHAPTER 25

THE NAME BARRY KANE DOES not apply to me for the next four days. Officially, I don't exist. I am a ghost, sent to kill and disappear. I can't even call my own brother by his name. He is designated as Number One. I am Number Two, but because my brother is kind of a dick, he calls me Shit. So I call him Piss.

The ghosts consist of five people in total, my brother as the team lead. I hold the demolition responsibility. Number Three is a computer expert fluent in Mandarin and Korean. Number Four is our sniper, and Five his spotter.

All of us wear ski masks, never to see each other's faces. I can only tell by their builds and eyes who they might be.

The snipers are roughly the same height, but I think the spotter is a woman. When I heard them talking, her voice had a strong foreign accent, possibly from Israel. The man had a strong southern accent, so I bet he is from Alabama. Number Three has a slim build and is only armed with a pistol.

John gives me these words of encouragement before we land, "Don't fuck up."

"Thanks…" *Jackass.*

We jump into a dark sky. The only light source is the nuclear facility miles away and that is a dim light. North Korea doesn't have much in the way of unnatural light. The few power plants are for powering military or government facilities.

I can't let my mind wander from focusing on my altimeter. The plane was at thirty-five thousand feet, and I have to pull my parachute at exactly one hundred feet. Not much of a gap. I got to do stuff like this in training years ago.

The ground is a fast approaching void. I can't look at it. I pull my parashoot the instant I can, jolting me to slow down. I land, deep snow half burying me. It takes me a while to dig myself out.

Parachutes packed, we rally. There can be no trace of us. We form up on Number One, then begin our hike to the target. A ten hour hike through the snow-covered mountains was the closest we could afford to drop.

We are to take out a nuclear missile station in North Korea. If we are caught, the orders are to kill ourselves. Each of us have been given a cyanide capsule to bite down on. Personally, that sounds too easy. If things get that bad, I'm going to use every bit of military-grade explosives to leave a crater in my wake.

The terrain is terrible. Jagged rocks no one has walked over in years. Number Three falls, letting out too much sound. We all stop and listen, in case anyone is around. Nothing. The only other sound is the wind cutting through the trees.

Number One asks, "Any damage?"

Number Three says, "No, just tripped on a root or something."

There is a slight metallic shine by their feet. "I don't think that's a tree." I brush away the snow and dirt to find a rotted M1 Garand rifle. "Must have been left over from the Korean War sixty years ago."

I think of how my grandfather's brother lost his life during that war. He was on rearguard while the rest of his battalion retreated during the Chinese advance. Apparently he was too young to fight in the second world war but was overjoyed when he was sent to Korea. The only picture of him is with my grandfather and Great Grandpa Jack just before he shipped out. It's the only time my grandfather smiled. He hadn't even when he opened his car dealership after the war.

We march on, unable to waste any time. I wish I could take the Garand with me, but the strap is broken and there is no way it is still in firing condition. It still would make a cool souvenir, but I can't be distracted with such things right now. Our exit ride will arrive exactly fifteen hours after we jumped. That won't give us much time to disable the radar and communications and cause a meltdown.

Eventually our target reaches our sights. Number Three is the only one who's tired. I worry they are actually a civilian. Must not be enough computer experts with multiple languages at the CIA.

The sniper team sets up along a ridge with a wide view of the compound.

Number One leaves his bag with them. "Deploy the sky hook thirty minutes before extraction."

We double-check to make sure our watches match. We have exactly four hours to complete the mission. There will only be a skeleton crew of twenty personnel operating the outpost. Normally, about one hundred personnel keep this remote eleven-acre base operational. Thanks to the time of year, about twenty have returned to their families while at least sixty will be sleeping at this hour, leaving a skeleton crew to protect the ten missile silos and five buildings, with at least one person in each of the four towers overlooking the perimeter. This place looks more like a prison than a military installation. However, if one person sounds an alarm, we'll have an entire enemy army upon us. How hard could it be?

We cut through the chain link fence at the far end. The metal is cheap aluminum. Grass is tougher than this. We take cover by one of the buildings where an anti-aircraft gun barrel sticks out the top. I check around the building and see two personnel with black AK-74U assault rifles, short barrels for building-to-building combat.

Both men look tired as they smoke cigarettes. They are shivering as they chat. With hand signals, I tell Number One. He acknowledges and responds with the signal to execute silently. We sneak up behind them, then in one motion, our knives go into their throats and we pull the corpses into the shadows. We take their keys and badges, which are used to enter a communications office, if intel was correct. All we need is direct access to the network here. The place is on a closed circuit to prevent hacking through the internet, but with direct input into the local network, they are vulnerable. Number Three inserts a USB connection from their laptop into an old desktop. Several loading screens pop up as the computer powers on.

Number Three says, "They need more RAM in these old things."

The computer shows another loading screen, then turns blue with a small black box. A few keystrokes later, Number Three says, "Radar and security cameras are off and all doors are unlocked. All phones are shut down, but the radios will still work. If I shut down the power, the next nearest base will be notified and we'll have enemy helicopters up our ass."

Number One says, "Number Two, go take out the radio tower. We'll proceed to the missile silo." Then into the radio he asks, "Overwatch, what is the hostile count?"

The southern voice replies, "I've bagged the four bogies in the towers and another four in the open."

The Israeli voice says, "I've counted six men entering the building next to the radio tower. And four have entered the barracks."

"That accounts for the twenty. Keep us posted if there are anymore." Then he turns to me. "You know what to do."

I say, "I always have." Then I run off.

As I make my way to the radio tower, Number Five informs me that my path is clear. I reach the tower, which stands two stories high. The bolts look rusty, so I probably only need two thermite charges to topple it, but I ain't getting paid to bring them back. So I plant one at each of the four legs.

I say into my radio, "Charges set."

This thing is going to make a lot of noise when it falls. I position myself behind some metal barrels with my suppressed M4 pointed at the building Number Four said six hostiles entered. The suppresser doesn't make the gun completely soundless, just muffles it so the sound doesn't travel.

Number One says, "Blow it and proceed to my position."

I do as commanded. The tower falls, completely cutting this facility off from the outside world.

Three hostiles rush out of the building. I end them with a few bursts before they have a chance to react. As one falls, his body holds the door open. I toss in a grenade just to be sure, then slowly move through the small space, into an armory with boxes stacked to make a table. Counting six bodies, looks like I interrupted their card game. I reload with my free moment. Soon I hear shouting from dozens of people moving with purpose. American regulations prevent soldiers from sleeping withing a hundred yards of the armory, but North Korea does not have regulations. There's going to be over fifty people sleeping in here. Damn army intel gave us the wrong building titles.

They can't call for help, but they could overpower us. I have to act fast. I pull the pins on two more grenades, tossing them down the hall at the approaching hostiles. Screams of pain are mixed into the explosions. I switch my gun to full auto as I turn the corner to cut down the charging hostiles. There's so many that I hardly aim. They try to move behind their bunkbeds, but there is no real cover. When I run dry, I reload as fast as possible. They take the opportunity to rush me, but I'm faster. Firing just as they fall onto me dead, I'm knocked down by the weight. They keep running at me, and I empty another magazine. Only a few remain. I try to reload, but one throws a full backpack at me, knocking the new magazine from my hand. One jumps at me, landing on me, and tries to strangle me. I take out my pistol and shoot him in the chest at point-blank range. As I pull the lifeless body off of me, I fire the last fifteen nine-millimeter rounds from my Beretta into the last hostiles.

I have to catch my breath before I stand up. The bodies of at least fifty people lie in this room of bunk beds. I reload both my pistol and rifle before doing one last burst on any possible survivors. Then I toss my last grenade into the room as I leave.

When I enter the missile silo, Number One is on a satellite phone and Number Three has their laptop plugged into the console. I lose focus, almost tripping on a man's corpse. He looks like just an employee, nonmilitary, possibly a janitor.

Number Three says, "It's ready to fire! Why are we holding?"

Number One holds his index finger up as someone speaks to him on the satellite phone. "Are you positive, sir? We won't get another chance at this, after the window closes."

This is a covert mission, with no outside radio contact. The satellite phone can reach anyone in the world. The team lead carries it as a last resort. Whoever John is talking to must be the one who authorized this mission. Could it be the president?

I move to a more strategic part of the room and peek at Number Three's laptop screen. Coordinates read "19.8968° N, 155.5828° W" and a second location "55.7558° N, 37.6173° E".

Are we actually launching two nuclear missiles? I thought this was sabotage to cripple a rouge nation's nuclear capabilities. I should be disgusted, but instead I am intrigued. Who are we destroying? Holy shit, I get to start World War III!

Number One says, "Cancel the launch. Fire the missile from within the silo. Set time for two hours. I want to be far away before this place is wiped off the map."

Number Three says, "That wasn't what I was promised."

Number One holds the phone out so Number Three can hear the speaker.

A voice cuts through the static. "The mission has changed. Don't make me waste an asset."

The voice has a slight accent. That's not the president. His tone paints a clear image of death if orders are disobeyed.

Number Three says with a hint of fear, "Understood."

My brother nods to me before hanging up the satellite phone. I understand exactly what he means. I keep my M4 pointed at Number Three's back, ready for any sudden moves.

What were you promised? I need to figure out those coordinates.

After a moment of typing, Number Three says, "It's done. I better still get everything else that was promised."

Number One looks over his laptop, confirming the work, then takes Number Three's pistol out of his holster and shoots him in the head. I watch as my brother places the pistol in Number Three's limp hand. It's a QSZ-92, a Chinese military pistol.

I say, "So he's the fall guy?"

My brother doesn't say anything, just takes the dead man's gear before leaving.

I call after him, "This place is about to be nuked. Ain't no point covering up evidence now."

He says, "We don't take risks."

We quickly make our way to the extraction point.

Number Four and Five already have the balloon in the air. They don't ask us about Number Three as we hook ourselves to the tether. Sky hook is supposed to work as a quick exit without landing a plane. A balloon is sent into the air and the plane grabs it with a hook, pulling a soldier directly into the air and then dragging him behind the plane. It was designed for one person at a time, but we don't have the time to wait. We are all secured to one thick rope with space between us, so we don't kick each other.

I hear a plane coming in low. Then in an instant, we are pulled upward. My stomach jolts worse than any time I've jumped out of an airplane as we are yanked straight into the air.

We are eventually winched into the AC-130 through the rear cargo door. My brother goes to the cockpit to talk to the pilots. Number Four and Five take a seat to decompress. I can't relax. I need to see the explosion. This is a once in a lifetime opportunity.

I stare out that window for over an hour, but I never see the light of the explosion. We're too far away.

Number Five says, "I love this job."

CHAPTER 26

SHADOW OF THE END

I AM WOKEN UP BY MY brother with a jab to my arm. "We're back, Barry."

I didn't realize how tired I was that I ended up sleeping for most of the thirteen-hour flight from North Korea, back to the secret base in the Nevada desert. It's dark out, and my watch says it's 2200 on December 13, 2012. We gained a day back, traveling across the ocean.

"Come on, Number Two."

After a stretch and a yawn, I say, "Right behind you."

Number Four and Five stay on the plane as large duffle bags are handed to them. Number Four yells to us as the plane refuels, "Pleasure doing business. Keep us in mind for the next one."

As we make our way across the airfield, I ask, "Were they all mercenaries?"

John checks to see if we're alone out here. "The team had to consist of people that could not be traced back to one particular country. That's why I needed you. I trust you without a doubt."

"But Number Four had an American accent. I'd bet he was from the south."

"He renounced his citizenship a long time ago. He's currently wanted by multiple governments for assassinations. He and his wife are useful for unconnected dirty work. Their trust goes as far as we can pay."

"What about Number Three?"

We stop just outside the main building. John looks around us again before he says, "I don't know what the official story will be. But we needed a fall guy. If you still want to know the answer, you can ask our superior during the debrief."

We finally take off our ski masks. I need to wash my face. I feel greasy. Then together we go to the third floor. We pass empty office cubicles and stop at the only occupied desk, where a secretary wears thick military-grade glasses. The poor bastard.

John asks, "Is he in?"

The secretary looks up from his computer. I can see the reflection of the cartoon show he was watching on his glasses. "Yeah…" He quickly takes off his headphones and closes the window on the computer. "Captain Johnathan Kane?"

"Yes."

"Go on in."

The office is large but modest, with no unused space. File cabinets, none taller than my shoulders, line all the walls. Windows overlook the airfield. Behind a simple desk sits a bald man typing on a desktop computer.

"Hello, gentlemen. Give me just a second to finish this."

John and I stand at ease in front of the desk. A map of

the world hangs over the cabinets. It's the same one from every history classroom, with longitude and latitude lines.

What were those coordinates Number Three had? There was one at about fifty-five degrees north, and thirty-ish something degrees east with some decimal points. I follow the latitude and longitude to Russia. Were we going to nuke Moscow?

China would have taken North Korea's side no matter what, and Russia would have eliminated North Korea with its automated defenses. We almost started a war between China and Russia.

What about the second missile? That had opposite coordinates. Roughly higher teens degree north, and a hundred fifty-five degrees west. I follow it to the middle of the Pacific Ocean and the only thing out there, the Hawaiian Islands. That would have given us an excuse to fight. Why did we cancel World War III? That would have been all the action I ever wanted.

The man at the desk is dressed in a black suit with a white shirt, his black tie hanging lose. When he finishes typing, I turn my attention back to him. Why does he have red eyes?

"Sorry about that. A lot has had to change today. I hear the mission was a success."

John says, "Yes, sir."

"Good. That will set North Korea's nuclear program back years, as well as the current power struggle over the latest death in the leadership. That pain will be out of mind for at least five years."

He looks at me. "And you must be Bartholomew Kane."

I say, "I am, sir."

He stands up and walks around the desk to shake my hand. "I'm always impressed by your family. Glad to have you on the team."

He's shorter than I am by two inches, but his grip his strong. I bet he could break my hand easily.

"How was the asset dealt with?"

John says, "Suicide by his own gun."

"Good. The official story will be that nuclear physicist Cho Jong planned to fire the missile, but the missile silo didn't open, destroying the facility. Enough evidence has been planted in his home to lead the North Korean Government to that conclusion. They may not let that information out of the country, but we know the truth. Correct, gentlemen?"

I nod as John again says, "Yes, sir."

"Excellent. Now if you two will excuse me, I have a lot more work to do. John, you're welcome to sleep in your office again, but please escort your brother off the premises. He is no longer needed here."

"But I'm just getting started," I say. "I'm ready for the next mission."

The man's voice grows stern. "Things have changed. You are not needed at this time. Return to your original destination. You will be called if needed."

John presses his hand into my back, pushing me to the door.

Then I notice something odd about the photos above the file cabinets. Most are in black and white. They are military photos that date back to the Civil War, based on the uniforms. The one that catches my eye in particular is of a man in a French Foreign Legion uniform with a white hat. A freshly sewn scar stretches from his cheek past his ear, and a second scar runs perpendicular from his eye down his cheek, and a third scar appears at the base of his eye. I'd know that apostrophe X anywhere.

I change direction, moving to pick up the picture frame and see the Colt pistol on his hip. Great Grandpa Jack. He stands next to a horribly scared man. Clearly they're friends as they pose for the picture. Great Grandpa's friend's entire face is scar tissue, as if he had healed from third-degree burns. There are multiple puffy scars around his neck. Are those from being cut or strangled? Even with all those scars, his oval eyes are unmistakable. This is the man giving me orders right now.

"How do you know my great grandfather?"

The man pauses before sitting back at his computer. He looks over to the picture, then says, "He was a good friend, who I miss every day. Captain, please escort your brother from this facility." He returns to typing. "That will be all."

That's it? I want more. You can't show me this side of adrenaline-fueled fighting and send me back to do nothing. I can't help looking over my shoulder, trying to see anything else I can as John ushers me to the door.

As we walk back to the elevator, John breaks the silence. "His eyes always creep me out a bit."

"They looked like goat eyes. What kind of freak buys contact lenses like that?"

"You saw the picture with Great Grandpa Jack. Those weren't fake. He's been alive for a long time. He's been close to the Kane family for generations."

We turn a corner to the barracks instead of the exit. "Before you go, I want to give you something." No one else is in the locker room as John opens his personal locker. "My life is about to be for someone else. And I don't want to sell this to someone who will keep it in a collection to never be driven again."

He hands me the keys to his Mustang. "Grandfather trusted it to me with the promise that I would keep it running at full throttle. I can't do that with a kid on the way."

I've wanted that car from the first moment Grandpa took us driving on the freeway. We reached ninety miles an hour. Joseph Kane cared for that car more than life itself. When he died in 2005 and gave it to John, I was filled with jealousy. Now, I finally have it. Yet, my life feels empty.

"When is the next mission?" I ask my brother.

John says, "There isn't one. That mission was a onetime deal. Desk work is more suited for a soon-to-be father."

"So this is it? An early Christmas gift and I go back to monotony? You just pull me into a world with an ancient man in charge of black ops that almost started World War III. You can't just send me packing now."

He forces the car key into my hand. "I'm sorry, little bro, but that's just how it works. Look at it this way. You now have a connection to the most powerful man on the planet. Your career can only go up from here."

"To what? The wars are ending. And we just canceled the next one. Uncle Rob was right, there is no glory for the second son."

"Uncle Rob is an addict with no ambition other than booze. Whatever he told you was bullshit. Take my car, clean yourself up, and I'll see you at Christmas."

He leaves me alone in the barracks. I look at my duffle bag of clothes in John's locker, because at the time, it was the best place to store it for the mission. I've gotten what I wanted, but it adds to nothing. I want to keep fighting, but I have no enemies to kill.

CHAPTER 27

NEW WORLD

"**I**, ANGEL LUNA MOLINA, HAVE changed the world!" I exclaim to Yabechun as I walk back and forth through the two floating spheres.

His face is impossible to read. I can't tell if he's upset or overjoyed. He doesn't smile, only asking, "How long can it last?"

That's a good question. I don't know. I have to flip through the notes on the reactors. "As long as they have power." I skim one of the pages. "Which is roughly a year. Then the reactors will need to be refueled. Any loss of power would sever the connection."

Yabechun says, "That will have to do." He turns to gives commands to his assistants. "Call up all experts on nuclear power. We need a reactor design that can be refueled and maintained without turning it off." He turns to another assistant. "Tell NASA the sky colonies on Venus are a go and to prepare for the terraforming of Mars." Then he raises his voice so everyone in the hangar can hear. "Have all weaponry and allied militaries prepare for an extraterrestrial response. I want to know if and when anything enters our solar system. I want to hit them before they can land. This is what you have trained for."

Everyone rushes off, leaving the two of us alone with two floating orbs behind me.

I ask, "What should I do? Is this the end of my employment?"

Yabechun says, "One moment please." He calls someone on his cell phone, lowering his voice.

I can't hear what he's saying until I get closer.

He says, "Don't make me waste the asset." A moment later he hangs up and turns to me. "It's far from the end of your employment. You're too valuable to be sent home. Follow me."

He leads me to an elevator in the back of a hangar, and we descend deep underground. He leads me through a series of rooms.

"This chamber was a cave discovered by miners following a silver deposit. Now it houses something far more valuable."

He swipes an ID badge against a console and types in a code as I angle myself to see the keypad. He typed in 1945. Five massive doors open, revealing what looks like maintenance chambers for circular aircraft.

My jaw drops. "No way! You guys really have UFOs."

Yabechun says, "UFOs means they are unidentified. These have been studied for years and we can identify them. They are spacecraft of no terrestrial origin." He gestures to an oval one that looks like a small airplane without wings but has two tail fins. "This one was found on an archaeological dig in the late 1800s. The acting government hid it from the world. It took fifty years till we could get it to fly. The rest of these have been stolen or bought from off-world sources."

This is amazing! Actual spacecraft. I need to touch at least one. I run up to one of the circular ones and run my hand across the smooth, cold metal. I want to fly it, but then I see a missile port. A clear addition of American technology.

"You don't have these to just study them, do you?"

"Of course not. These are the only thing keeping our backward planet alive. Each one of these can be fitted with a nuclear payload and deployed within minutes of a credible threat. We are not the only ones in this galaxy, and the others have all been around a lot longer than us. If they really wanted something from us they could take it.

"These five ships, plus the three in Russia and the two in China are deterrents. The threat of ten hydrogen bombs being delivered straight to their most populated centers is enough to keep our enemies at bay. Thankfully, for most of current history, we haven't had anything they really wanted. But that has all changed as of today."

"What?" Fear swallows me. I feel very small next to these things. "What have I done?"

Angel's Window was meant to stop the third world war. I was destined to save millions of lives.

Yabechun says, "You have saved us from being forever trapped on one planet. We have no means of replicating the power sources. The limited supply we have can be used to briefly train pilots for a singular possible mission. The element needed was mined out of all reachable sources long before humans walked the Earth. But now we have something unique. Something the lords of our galaxy have never come close to in their millions of years of control."

He places his hand on my shoulder, which only makes me feel smaller. "Before your invention, my plan was to control the population through war. A cruel reboot of human society. Now we will need every single person to fight alongside each other. One united front for all of humanity as we expand into the cosmos."

Oh God, Jason was right. "You were going to cause a world war. How could you?"

His grip tightens, strong enough to get his point across. "Our technology has become stagnant, causing more damage to our planet than power generation. War forces innovation. In addition, Earth can handle only a limited population. A cleansing of the weak is necessary. I need to maintain a veteran population."

I say, "You are pure evil!"

He lets go, unfazed by my words. "Of course I am. But I am *necessary* evil. Without my actions, humanity would have been destroyed sixty years ago. I was there, child, when humanity gave up its freedom."

His voice grows crueler. "I am old, very old. I have seen tens of thousands of battles. I have killed many with my own hands. I have founded nations and watched the fall of Rome. I witnessed the combination of technology with industry in the first world war and the loss of an entire generation for a pointless cause. I was there when the first atomic bomb dropped. That was the day human technology became capable of planetary destruction. Every action I take is cruel, but I do it all in the hope of securing the future."

I need to get away from this man. I need to get to my family. I run to the elevator that brought us down. In an instant, he is next to me. I press my back to the wall, pushing the up button repeatedly.

He says, "You do realize that you have become the most valuable person on the planet. I can't let you leave."

He sees me pressing the up button. "You're in the middle of the desert. The is nowhere to run to." He swipes his badge over the console on the wall and places it in his pocket, then grabs my hand and pulls me into the elevator. "Understand this, Angel. You are too valuable to leave these premises until I can reveal your technology to the world. When that time comes, you will be compensated to a life of absolute luxury. Until then, calm yourself! I know you're used to living in confined places. You will be fine."

I like the sound of luxury, but one question sits heavy in my head. "Can I see my family?"

He leans down to my level, looking me directly in the eye. "Not anymore."

I say the greatest lie of my life. "I understand."

He backs off. "Good."

We reach the ground floor. Several soldiers guide me to the room I was provided with when I was first brought to this facility. I actually forgot I had my own room in the barracks. I've spent all my time in the hanger, building my Window.

I am left alone.

How the hell am I going to get out of here? I take a deep breath. I've spent many years of my life in prison. I know them like the back of my hand. The first gate is the walls you put up in your own head, where you accept that you're not going anywhere. Not this time. I need to get home to my family. The room is on the ground floor, but the window is too small to slip out of.

Wait, I'm overreacting. I can just call them to check in. What are their phone numbers? Mom doesn't have a cell phone, can't afford the payments, and Francisco puts all excess income into his car. I could call Renato, but he's sitting in Tent City for the next several years. I fear the worst has become of them. Yabechun would gladly sacrifice millions of people if he believed it was necessary. He could have done something terrible to secure this new technology by eliminating all other evidence. I have to bust out of here.

I analyze my door for alarm triggers. I carefully open it, and nothing happens. Instead, I find a man in uniform guarding my door. He only has a pair of handcuffs on him.

He asks, "Do you need anything?"

"No." Then I close the door.

Of course, it couldn't be that simple. I'll have to bide my time. He's not going to stand there all day. I'll grab a nap now, then wait until he takes a bathroom break. He's only human. I can survive in an enclosed room for years.

The sun rises and sets. I've watched his boots from the tiny crack under the door. His feet move uneasy, as if he's uncomfortable. Not much time left now. The moment he walks in one direction, I make my move in the opposite direction, closing the door silently and speed walking away.

The main area of the barracks has a bunch of lockers but is devoid of personnel and cameras. I casually stroll out, but this feels too easy. I see someone in the barracks and immediately step back down the hall I came from. I peek out, exposing as little of myself as possible. The man is changing into civilian clothing. Must be easier to clean up on base than at home. I bet he's going home for the day. It's got to be past nine at this point. Either way, he's my ticket out of here.

I have maybe a minute or two of preparation. I need something so I can blend in. Yabechun is most likely preparing everyone for his plan of a new world. I have to act quickly and as if I belong. So my main obstacle will be security cameras. There is a fatal flaw I can exploit. Most camera monitors are only watching for routine movement, so no running. They may know what I look like, but most cameras are low resolution. Government facilities always hire the lowest bidder. I just need to change my outward appearance and put on a hat to avoid direct view of my face. They will be able to figure out where I went, but I'll have a head start.

Most of the lockers don't have locks. I grab a military jacket that's a little big and a camo hat similar to a baseball cap, which I pull down over my face. I know I look sketchy, with my beat-up jeans and old sneakers. Anyone paying attention will notice. God, I hope this works.

The man finishes changing. He looks young, maybe twenty years old. He combs his dirty blond hair back. This white boy has clearly been in a fight. He has small scars on the upper half of his face. He puts in some ear buds and turns up the volume before he lifts a large sack of stuff as he leaves. I calmly walk behind him, maintaining a solid thirty feet of distance between us. My footsteps are light, while his boots make thuds. The halls are completely empty.

What the hell have I done? I can't think about that now. My priority is to get home. I fear it might be gone.

The man goes out to a small parking lot. I slip through the door just before it closes. The parking lot has four cameras on every light pole. There is no way someone is watching this many cameras very closely. Probably there's one overworked person just kind of paying attention. The lot is surrounded by a tall fence topped with razor wire. It'd be too difficult to climb out in the dark and with nothing but desert to run to. There is a guard structure at the gate. The man inside has his feet up, reading a book with a colorful cover. When your facility is this far from everything, you become complacent.

The man I'm following unlocks a red and black Mustang, then throws his duffle into the trunk, closing it without locking it. I have to time this right. Just as he sits into his car and closes his door, I slip into the trunk, closing it softly without it clicking closed. This thing is too old to have a trunk release, so I hold it closed. I used to smuggle drugs in my dad's car. Now, I'm smuggling myself. This is a weird feeling.

The car backs out, then stops. Muffled talking follows, but it sounds calm. I don't think they saw me. Then comes the clanking of an opening gate followed by the car moving forward.

I made it out! That almost feels too easy.

The car picks up speed. On a bumpy road, I try to hold onto something as I am thrown around. The duffle bag hits me and almost makes me lose my grip on the trunk. I do not want to fly out right now. The road smooths out, and the car speeds up.

What the hell kind of a mad man is driving?

I hear intense heavy metal music. We must be on the freeway. He's definitely way over the speed limit.

Hold on. I'll be home soon.

CHAPTER 28

BARRY'S CHOICE

I T IS IMPOSSIBLE NOT TO push the pedal to the metal in John's Mustang. I should say *my* new Mustang. I like the sound of that. "Barry's Mustang."

No, it needs a more nuanced name. Something that says power and speed. "Lightning…Speed Lightning." I don't think I'll be giving back Speed Lighting.

I've got to stop for gas soon. I got too caught up in the music mixed with the roar of the engine and made the six-hour drive from the middle of Nevada to Phoenix Arizona in less than five hours.

No point in going to Yuma anymore with Mom and Dad moving to DC this week. I should talk to my little brother. Should I steer Austin away from the path I took? It's been nothing but bullshit after bullshit. He won't understand until he sees it for himself. Austin has to make his own decisions. He's smart. I'm sure he'll figure it out. However, he is ambitious and that will take him in dangerous directions. I just want to get to Texas as check in, then drink myself into a coma.

Should I ask for Dad's help back to the action? Wait… does Dad know the man with red eyes? He probably introduced John to him. That was the push he was talking about. That's how Dad went from a high school dropout to a goddamned General. What kind of mission did Dad do for him? Are those really tiger scars, or from something else? How come they get the real action, while I'm stuck with bullshit?

I pull into a gas station on the northern edge of Phoenix along Interstate 17. While the tank fills, I clean dead bugs from the windshield. I hate mosquito season.

The trunk pops open.

What the hell? Did John give me a broken car?

Then a Hispanic teenager rolls out, drenched in sweat, trying to catch his breath. He looks around to orient himself, then sees me.

We stare at each other in silence for a full minute. I honestly don't know how to respond right now. Is he an illegal immigrant who hopped in my car for a free ride? That makes no sense. I just drove nonstop from a top secret military base in the middle of actual nowhere. Plus, the trunk was empty when I put my bag in there before I left.

The teen speaks first. "You drive like a fucking mad man. You know, the speed limit exists for a reason."

You little shit. "Oh, I'm sorry. I was unaware I had a stowaway! Who the fuck are you, and why were you in my car?"

He says, "Well, it's kind of a funny story…" He's shifting his weight to his back foot.

I start to say, "Hold on," but he sprints away. I run after him.

He only makes it a few yards before I catch up to him,

shoulder-checking him into a rusty fence and then pinning him against it with my forearm across his chest. He struggles, but he's no match for me.

I yell, "I'm only going to ask this one time before I get mean. Who are you?"

He calms down. "I'm the man who changed the world and gave absolute power to the man with red eyes." There is no emotion on his face, just a blank expression.

"Oh shit…" What the hell did I just get involved in?

I already know too much. I think I just gave them a reason to eliminate me. I need to get out of here. I need to get as far away from here as possible. I need to go off the grid. I'll ditch the car and make my way to the border. I'll keep heading south until I can't anymore. I can find work in a mine in Chile. I'll completely vanish from the world.

"Wait, if you just gave that man absolute power, why would you need to escape?"

He hesitates. Fighting back tears, he says, "I need to know if he killed my family."

Why am I in this situation? I hear "Bad Luck Barry" being whispered in the back of my head. God damn it! I can't just leave this kid here. I doubt that would be the better option. So I ask the dumbest question of my life. "Where is your family?"

He says, "I'd know these hills anywhere. We're in Phoenix, aren't we? They're in the Vagabond Mobile Home Park in Alhambra."

That's not far, just off the interstate. "I'll take you there. But after I drop you off, we forget we ever met. I'm not becoming a target because of your actions."

We get back into my car. I take the battery out of my

cell phone. It can't be tracked if there's no power in it. I still have plausible deniability. I did not knowingly help the kid escape. I'm just taking him home.

I ask no questions as we drive. I don't want to know any more than I do. It doesn't take us long to get there, but each minute feels like an eternity. Red lights take a lifetime as I feel a team of assassins will come out of nowhere.

As we enter the RV park, I smell a familiar scent. "There was a fire here recently."

The teen tells me to stop at the burned remains of a mobile home surrounded with yellow tape.

To the kid's credit, he doesn't cry. He just plainly says, "I knew it. That fucking monster got my notebook by force. He got me out of Juvie by the same methods. Eliminate the problem to secure your solution."

He gets out and walks over to a tree where several holes have been dug into the ground. Then he drops to his knees and picks up an oil-stained shirt.

"You goddamn son of a bitch. Why did you give me this knowledge? I never wanted this." He's crying now. "Why did you take them from me? They had nothing to do with any of it. All I wanted was to give them a better life."

I should drive away. This isn't my problem anymore. He can get help from a neighbor. But where's the fun in that? I want action, and what would provide more action than going directly against the man with red eyes?

I ask the boy, "What are you going to do about it?"

The kid stands up. "I'm going to expose Yabechun to the world. I'm going to destroy everything he has built. Then I'll kill my former friend." The kid is shaking with anger.

I walk over to him. "I understand your rage better than

anyone," I say. "But I can tell by how you carry yourself, you've never killed. I know what it means to end a life with my own hands. I'll help you."

"Why?" He wipes away his tears.

With pride I say, "Because I am a Kane. I'm a killer. It's my family's curse. It's about time I finally got to use it."

The kid hands me the ruined shirt. "Avenge them." Then he gets back in the car.

On the drive back to Area 51 in Nevada, the kid says his name is Angel Molina Luna. He tells me his life story over the full six-hour drive. He tells me about his teleportation device, how he was given the mathematical formulas to build it by a friend in Juvie who claimed to be from the future. I don't know how much is true, but he wouldn't have escaped Area 51 for nothing.

After a while, my mind drifts. I'm about to do something extremely stupid. I need to prepare. I have no weapons, plus, I bet they know exactly where we are. I'll have to wing it on instincts.

The only reason they haven't unleashed the full power of their influence to catch us is probably because we are heading right to them. I have to act as if I'm doing the patriotic thing. I have to act in full support of them, then strike at the most opportune moment. My actions will have to be cold and quick. I move my wristwatch above my thumb because it'll hit harder than my knuckles.

I put the battery back into my phone and set it to voice recording. My phone is cheap, so it can record only a minute of video, and we'll need more than that. I give the phone to Angel and tell him to start the recording as soon as we reach the base.

At the turnoff from the freeway, my heart starts pounding. *Just breathe,* I tell myself. I can do this. I *will* do this. *Just breathe. Just breathe.*

There are no patrols, and we are waved through the gates by the same guard as when I left. It looks like he's almost finished his book. We are expected. I've never been this nervous before.

Just breathe…

I will kill the man with red eyes. I know he's over a hundred years old to have fought in the first world war. I'll have to catch him off guard.

When we stop in the main parking lot, we're immediately surrounded by military police, all with Beretta pistols drawn, the older model. They're behind on their weaponry. The rest of the military has upgraded to Glocks. They shout, "Step out of the vehicle with your hands up!"

I say to Angel, "Move slowly and do what they say. When I make a move, you make a run for whatever kind of evidence you can get."

"You got it."

I'm a fighter. It's what I was raised to be. I know my chances out in the open are bad. There's not enough cover, and attackers may be far out of my range. I need to get inside, where I can use their numbers against them.

We make no sudden movements as we step out of the car with our hands in the air. They relax just slightly, then pat us down for weapons, not noticing the placement of my watch. Why would they? Their primary security problems are civilians trying to catch a glimpse of behind the curtain, not anyone with real malice.

As they lead us into the facility, I keep track of every

turn and stairwell we take. I force everything to memory, because I'll need it for what is to come. We are led to a conference room where the man with red eyes is examining a map of the stars with what looks like a foreign language marking different sections. Two MPs come in with us, one taking up position at the door while the other stands behind Angel and me as we face Yabechun.

I say, "Yabechun, I brought you back the kid."

Yabechun rests his hands in his pockets and smiles as his eyes remain on the map. "I see. So little Angel has told you everything?"

I have to keep my answer as close to honest as possible. "I want to be on the winning side." *My side.*

Yabechun turns to us, his eyes locking on me. "Good answer. I really want to believe you." He turns his focus to Angel. "So you went home. Now, I know you're upset, but you need to understand. We can't afford loose ends. The dead tell no tales. This is the cost of ensuring humanity's survival. Understand this, every star in the sky holds the possibility for sustaining life on three planets. Same as ours, and each planet's civilization achieved intergalactic travel long ago. We are just barely scratching the possibilities. Each star harbors a threat that could easily wipe us out. Don't be a fool. The human race needs you."

Angel lifts his hand out with his middle finger raised. "Fuck you!"

Yabechun shifts, taking his hands out of his pockets. "You got out because security wasn't paying attention. Because the guard I assigned you took a bathroom break without getting a replacement. That mistake will never happen again. You will be watched every second. It's a shame. You could have lived a comfortable life, but I will do what is needed."

I don't want to hear more of his monologue. I strike the man behind me, pressing my hardened fist into his throat. As he falls back, blood spurting from his mouth, I pull his pistol from its holster. Switching the gun off safety, I put two rounds into the guard at the door. I turn my focus to Yabechun, expecting him to be charging me, but he merely stands.

He gently raises his hands, looking more relaxed than ever, and says, "You better make it count."

I take a quick breath, gaining control of my adrenaline, and fire a bullet right at his heart.

CHAPTER 29

RUN

I DUCK AS BARRY TAKES DOWN the guards. My ears ring with pain from the gunshots. The guard with an indented throat struggles to breathe. I know I should help, but I've never seen someone this close to death before. I need to think of my own survival right now. I take the extra gun magazines from his belt and his security badge. We are going to have to blast our way out of here.

Barry fires again.

Yabechun remains standing as a bullet falls off his chest, leaving a tiny tear in his shirt.

The only words I can manage are, "Oh shit."

Barry shoots him two more times in the chest and once in the head. Each bullet ricochets into the wall.

The monster stands unfazed before he sighs, "Such a waste of ammo." He steps toward Barry. "Waste of a good shot too."

Barry keeps his breathing calm and fires one more bullet into Yabechun's right eye. The eye pops as the bullet lodges itself in the socket.

Yabechun shoves his finger into his eye socket to fish out the bullet.

Then Barry puts a bullet into the other eye.

Yabechun shouts, "You insignificant fool! You won't leave here alive!"

Barry mutter's something before he grabs me by my arm and pulls me out of the room. We run through the halls. I am completely lost, but Barry seems to know where to go. We stop at a staircase.

He says, "Get to Yabechun's office on the third floor. Take the stairs down the hall. Grab whatever evidence you can. Get to the car. I left the key in the ignition. There's enough gas to get to the nearest town. Don't wait for me! I'll buy you as much time as I can."

Barry pulls a nearby fire alarm.

I grab him before he runs off. "Wait!" I hand him the ammo I took from the dying guard. "I owe you so much."

He says, "Honestly, Angel, this isn't about you. I didn't join the army out of my family's obligation. I joined because I wanted to cause damage." Then he runs off, and soon I hear a dozen gunshots.

How the hell am I going to find one office in a massive complex full of locked doors and military personnel? I very much stand out as a teenager in sweaty clothes. At the third floor, I run into a locked door. Where did I put that ID card?

As I pull out the card, the door bursts open. I hide in the gap between the open door and the wall and watch a dozen people run out. They're arguing about whether the alarm is for an active shooter or a fire. When shots echo from far away, one of the personnel says, "Either way, I'm not sticking around to find out." They all agree and rush down the stairs.

I swing around and slide through before the door closes, finding myself alone on this floor. I assume the office I need will most likely be the largest one. He'd want to look over the base. So I search for the largest office where I swipe the stolen key card and type in 1945. The door unlocks, and I slip in.

The room is large with file cabinets lining the side walls and black and white pictures on all of them. One of the pictures is of Yabechun shaking hands with President Obama. This is definitely his office.

A small desk with a desktop computer on it sits in the center of the room.

Now, what the heck am I looking for? Maybe files with Top Secret stamped on them. Or perhaps I should just steal his computer and find a way to hack it later. I know I don't have enough time to do a deep search. I begin unplugging the desktop from under the desk.

Then I hear his voice. "Do you honestly think you can escape again?"

I can't fight him, and I can't outrun him. *Come on, brain, think.* I raise the computer above my head. "If you come any closer, I'll smash all the information you have in here to nothing."

Yabechun stands in front of the door, carelessly playing with two bullets in his hand. "Smashing it will only give the poor IT department a bad day as they put the pieces back together." He calmly approaches me.

I try to back up but bump against the window. There's nowhere left to go.

He places the two bullets on his desk. "This could have been far easier. You need to understand that everything I do is for the good of humanity. All sacrifices are small in the grand scheme as we move forward."

I throw the computer at him and sprint for the door.

He catches the computer with one hand and grabs my collar with the other. I almost choke. He places the computer next to the bullets, then with little effort, he tosses me against his office window, which shakes but doesn't crack.

He says, "You should have stayed put and accepted my hospitality." He takes me by the hair and guides me out of the office. "Now you're going to watch the consequences of starting a fight you can't win."

CHAPTER 30

DAMAGE

I CAN FINALLY PUT AWAY EVERYTHING that makes me human. Don't call me Barry. Call me Devil. All that matters now is causing damage. They are not human beings working a job. They are targets. I know deep down that I won't make it out of this, but that's the point. I am a Kane, a true killer, and I will kill everyone on this base.

The fire alarm continues to ring as the intercom announces, "Warning: active shooter. Warning: active shooter on base."

That's right, come and get me. I'm ready.

I gun down everyone I see. I don't want to spare any of them. I have to pull all attention away from Angel. He has to expose this place for what it truly is.

A man with a rifle rounds the corner in front of me and lifts the gun, but in one quick motion, I yank the barrel and fire my pistol into his face.

Someone yells from down the hallway, "There he is!"

With my new rifle in hand, I take cover. Bullets rip into the wall. I use this next thirty seconds to check the ammo in the M16 assault rifle, make sure there is a round in the chamber, and salvage the dead man's vest with four loaded magazines in it. It's a shame it lacks any means to stop bullets. Then with my body protected by the wall, I stick the rifle out and blind fire back with a few bursts.

I'm clearly facing untested security. They've only ever played soldier, never really been in the shit. If they had actually been in combat, they would have returned fire from cover or advanced while keeping me under pressure. Instead, they stood in the open, wasting ammo. My blind fire hit two of them. The third had never seen someone killed or wounded before, so he stands frozen, allowing me to aim from cover and end him.

A wounded one lies on the ground holding his gut as blood seeps out. He tries to grab his gun, and I see the panic in his eyes. I smile as I put a bullet in his head. This is too easy. I salvage more ammo before advancing through the base.

Bodies lie everywhere. This has been fun. How could they be this unprepared for an inner assault?

It doesn't matter. I need to make sure Angel has escaped. I return to the main entrance to see if he has taken the car yet, peeking out from behind cover. Military vehicles have been arranged to form a barricade. They're planning a counterattack. I don't have much time left. My car is exactly where I left it. Angel hasn't gotten out yet. Something has gone wrong. I need to buy more time.

I move to a room with a window and prop it open just enough to point my barrel out, because shooting through glass would ruin my shot. I'll only have a few shots before they return fire. Killing someone will eliminate only one enemy, but if I wound one, then at least two others will be forced to help. There's one clearly giving orders to several others positioned behind the vehicle barricade.

I hold a deep breath, focusing the iron sight on his right pectoral region. The shot hits his shoulder, knocking him off his feet. As others scramble, I fire more bursts at leg height. Then I slip away as they return fire on an empty window.

That bought me maybe five or ten minutes as they deal with wounded and find a new commander and launch a counteroffensive. It's all I can do for now. I run at full speed to the stairs, praying I don't run into the man with red eyes. If he's not outside prepping a counterattack, then he's still inside. Did he get to Angel?

I rush to the stairs, not checking my corners. I don't have the time, not for anything. As I reach the door, someone drives me into the wall with immense force. My body feels crushed, but it wasn't enough to make me drop my rifle. I can't angle it to shoot, so I slam the stock into his ribs. He winces but holds on. I swing again, and this time he moves to block, allowing me to break free. I try to adjust my gun to shoot, but he grabs the barrel, turning it away. I see the determination on my brother's face.

John pleads, "Stop this, Barry!"

I say, "No!"

His palm uppercuts my chin. My legs weaken, and my rifle drops to the floor.

No! I will not go down so easily. I brace my legs, pivoting as I throw a straight punch to his nose, which cracks. Pain erupts at my ribs from his next blow. We stand face to face, exchanging punches. I will not hold back.

I duck under his punch as I jump back, reaching for the

pistol tucked into my belt in the back of my pants. "No one to stop us this time," I say.

He sees the gun and grabs my hand before I can fire. His other hand grabs my throat. I kick out one of his legs, causing us both to fall, but his grip only tightens. He's trying to kill me. He slams my hand against the floor, causing me to fire off a round. With another hit, I drop the pistol. He squeezes my throat. I can't breathe. I kick him between his legs. His grip loosens but not enough to escape, only enough for me to tuck my chin under his forearm. I turn and bite off a chunk of his hand and then push him back. I smack him in the ear. He winces but wraps his arm around my throat. I fight his grip with one hand and with the other I grab his face. A couple of fingers find his mouth. Hooking his cheek with my fingers and pulling back, I feel his cheek start to rip. I slip my head out as soon as he moves to prevent more of damage.

I reach for my pistol with my left hand, but John stomps my fingers, breaking several of them. Then his knee slams into my head. I'm dazed, but I can't give him any space. I dive into him, and we fall back to the floor. I punch with my good hand and broken one.

"I won't lose to you!" I scream as we stagger to our feet.

He catches my damaged hand and squeezes the broken fingers, following that by punching my elbow inward. It snaps. With my good arm, I grab his shirt collar and slam my forehead into his nose. He's dazed, so I do it again, and his blood splashes onto my face.

In one quick action, he punches me in the throat with one arm. Then his other hand grabs my face digging his thumb into my left eye. I pull back, but he presses forward and punches my face until my eye pops in my skull. I do the same to him, popping his eye out of the socket with my thumb. He doesn't give an inch, so I kick his knee outward with all my malice. His thumb leaves my eye socket as we fall once again.

Breathing hard, we stare at each other. My brother has only one eye and blood runs from his crushed nose, torn cheek, and dislocated eyeball. With only one arm, I know I have to finish this now.

Both my guns lie not too far away. It's four feet to the pistol and a little farther for the rifle. I jump for my pistol. John already knows what I'm going for and kicks me hard in the ribs, doing more damage to his injured leg to knock me away from the pistol, but I land next to my rifle.

John yells, "That's enough, Bartholomew Kane!" My brother is propping himself up against the wall with one leg as he points the pistol at me with his left hand. "Don't make me do it."

I say, "You know, I won't give you a choice. I ain't going out by the needle like Aunt Rosemary."

He yells, "You god damn idiot! You think your actions are justified? There's more at stake than your fucking ego!"

"You got your glory. I took mine today."

"It's never been about the glory. It's about the *mission*."

I lunge for my rifle.

John fires.

Heat burns through my chest. All my muscles tense. I can't hear my heartbeat. I can't hear anything. The world is so quiet. Everything falls away into nothing.

CHAPTER 31

ANGEL'S TRUTH

I AM FORCED TO WATCH AS a soldier shoots Barry in the chest. The soldier has a face almost identical to Barry's.

Yabechun says, "Good job, Kane."

The soldier slowly slides to the floor and lets out an exhausted, "Thank you, sir."

My head is released, but I don't move. There's no point. We failed. I'm going to stay here for the rest of my life.

Looking over the scene, Yabechun says, "The cost of tomorrow is paid for by the corpses of today. We kill, we eat, we move forward. Things can no longer be simple. We have to accept responsibility of the cost." He turns to me. "I know you're sad about your family, but look at the dead around you. Will the death of all these people bring them back? I thought you were smart. Each one of them had families and friends that loved them."

I think about all the people Barry killed to help me. Fear has left me, as well as all hope. "I'm not smart."

"Maybe, but thanks to you, humanity can claim its place among the stars."

All this death because of me. "I didn't do anything. The equations were given to me by someone else."

Yabechun freezes, glaring down at me.

This is all Jason's fault. He gave me those equations with the full knowledge of the future. I say, "Jason Baker taught me those equations. He's a terminal patient I met back in Juvie." *I hope your illness is as painful as possible, you son of a bitch.*

"So he's not dead yet. I'll have a chat with him."

"He has a brain tumor. There's nothing you can do."

The man with red eyes smiles. "You should be terrified by what I can do."

"Can you save him?"

"If he really does hold value."

I smile for the first time in what feels like forever. "Good." Save him and bring him into the fold, so he can lose everything as I have. Then when he's at his lowest, I'll kill him as painfully as possible.

This is your fault, Jason. You should have just died.

TO BE CONTINUED

⟨◆⋅◆━◆◆◆⟩

Thank you for reading! I hope you enjoyed the story and will stay tuned for the next story in the End of Earth series. Please visit your favorite online retailer and leave a review. I look forward to reading your feedback!

ACKNOWLEDGMENTS

Most importantly, thank you to Leon Unruh for being my primary editor on this book. Your guidance and feedback helped me make this story possible.

Thank you again to my friend Michael Miller, the Lucky Warlord, for providing me with your firsthand war experiences to help my story sound more realistic.

Thank you to my friend of many years, Charlie, for providing me with your insight of how prisons actually work. I should have come to you sooner for the first book.

Thank you again to my Aunt Maureen Simons for helping me with the second step of this story.

Thank you Debra L. Hartmann for helping me finish this book.

As always, thank you to my friends and family for your constant support.

Finally, thank you, Dolton Spencer. Your knowledge of runes helped me name one of the most important characters of this story.

I wanted to bring a bit of reality into my work of fiction this time, in the hope that we can better understand it all as we move into the future. Here are the story plots that took inspiration from real events and people:

Hudson's injury in chapter 14 is inspired by the real American hero, Sgt. Dan Powers. He was stabbed in the head with a knife while on deployment in Iraq and survived, having the knife removed and then continuing to serve in the US military.

Also mentioned in chapter 14 is an American soldier captured by the Taliban. This was meant to be a reference to Bowe Bergdahl who was held by the Taliban for five years. In 2009, Army Rangers did a number of operations to find him but were not successful. Bergdahl was eventually released in 2014, but that is a very long and complicated story.

In Chapter 18, the raid on the high-ranking al-Qaeda terrorist is inspired by an operation in April of 2010 by the Iraqi Special Operation Forces backed by US troops. The operation killed ISIS leaders Abu Ayyub al-Masri and Abu Omar al-Baghdadi and arrested sixteen others. A US Blackhawk helicopter was shot down, killing a Ranger NCO and wounding the aircrew.

Of course, the wars in Afghanistan and Iraq are real conflicts with long, complicated histories and America's involvement has only recently ended. The wounds of the conflict are still fresh. I want to thank those who have given their lives to this country in the hope of something better.

Thank you. May we never forget.

ABOUT THE AUTHOR

Matt Simons carried the story that would one day become The End of Earth around in his head ever since he was a little kid. The story morphed and evolved through the years, eventually becoming what it is now. All it took was a global pandemic and being trapped in quarantine to start really writing it.

A man with a sense of humor that does not exclude himself, Matt Simons is known among friends and family by his nickname, Nightstand, which he earned while carrying a nightstand down three flights of stairs and across two blocks before realizing it was nearly killing him because it was full of weights. The heavy lesson learned: check the contents of what you will carry around before lifting it.

Let's connect on social media!
Instagram: https://www.instagram.com/nightstand_matt/
Twitter: Nightstand Matt at
https://twitter.com/MattSim55879370